Other books by Kimberly T. Matthews

THE PERFECT SHOE

NINETY-NINE AND A HALF
JUST WON'T DO

BEFORE I LET GO

A LITTLE HURT AIN'T
NEVER HURT NOBODY

GOOD MONEY

KIMBERLY T. MATTHEWS

URBAN BOOKS
www.urbanbooks.net

This is a work of fiction. Any references or similarities to actual events, real people, living or dead, or to real locales are intended to give the novel a sense of reality. Any similarity in other names, characters, places, and incidents is entirely coincidental.

URBAN SOUL is published by:

Urban Books
6 Vanderbilt Parkway
Dix Hills, NY 11746

ISBN-13: 978-1-59983-093-3
ISBN-10: 1-59983-093-0

First Printing: May 2009
10 9 8 7 6 5 4 3 2

Printed in the United States of America

ACKNOWLEDGMENTS

I really had to struggle to write this piece, not because people aren't worthy of thanks or mentioning, but because there are greater ways they have impacted my life that have little to do with this book coming into fruition. So listing them here would be typical and run-of-the-mill.

Almost everybody thanks God, their parents, their spouse, their pastor and first lady and their children, and their wonderfully fantastic editor. And their sorority sisters and their real sisters—sometimes the brothers get thanked too. Then the person who read their novel fifty times and either gave feedback or cried. Then the person who encouraged them to go forward and write their book when they couldn't think of another single word. Then the person who made them stay on task, or loaned them a computer when their laptop blew up, or picked up their daughter from cheerleading practice so that the book could get done. There's the family that had to eat frozen pizzas and TV dinners so that the author could be locked away in a room writing—and had to get meals slid in under the crack of the door. Then the people who have bought or at least promised to buy a book in the past. Oh yeah—the book club that read the last book and let them come over and eat cheese squares.

Anyway, the people that are deserving of thanks deserve thanks for other things, not so much because I wrote this book. So since I have to say thank you to somebody somewhere, let me start with the people who really did make it happen.

Hmmm . . . well, nobody brought me peanut butter sandwiches so I wouldn't have to cook. Nobody offered to babysit my fantastic nephew, so he wouldn't bombard me with a thousand questions (or give me the extended version of how he spent his day at the summer program—or ask me to read folded-up squares of white paper stapled together, scribbled with pencil, which he proudly called his comic book—or look at his latest LEGO sculpture) while I was trying to concentrate on writing. Nobody read it in part and said, "Girl, this is good! You need to write this!" My pastor, as awesome as he is—doesn't even know about this book. Neither does his wife. I don't have any sorority sisters. My real sisters and brother? Please! They don't really read my books—but that's okay because I don't read their stuff either. Nobody preread it other than the content editor (and I will talk about her in a minute). My sons—with their handsome selves—they didn't help me either, so no point in thanking them. My Perfect Shoe of a fiancé? You would think I could at the least say thanks to him, but uh-uh! He was sooooo busy spoiling me with dinners and dates, and flowers and candy, and diamond earrings and foot rubs, and—and—and all the things that a woman loves—it was hard to tell him to go away to let me work. So he gets no thanks either. Not for this.

So, what it boils down to is this:

God—He is always and forever deserving of a million thanks in every single situation—good and bad. So as typical as that sounds, I cannot and will not fail to thank Him.

Of course a great editor is an absolute must—and that credit goes to Nicole Peters. Nicole made me change the point of view and it was killing me! Well, she didn't *make* me, but what author doesn't have sense enough to follow the content editor's recommendations? Still—Lord have mercy on my soul—Nicole had me struggling. But hey, I got it done. Nicole gave me other solid feedback too—which I applied . . . I think. I had to or else you wouldn't be reading this. So, thanks, Nicole!

And Shandra Bradford—who constantly burst into my office excited to know what was going on with these characters, and physically acted out what needed to be going on with them when I really didn't know.

And to everyone who let me borrow their name—first or last—which you didn't even know about!

And to everyone who has *ever* bought a book that I wrote. I hope you bought this one and you didn't just borrow it from a friend. If you did, I'm not talking about you. I take that back, yes, I am. Thank you too!

All right—I think I'm done now. If I left you out, it was probably on purpose. Next time, come offer to babysit or boil a hot dog or something!

Kim

PS: Nicole made me write this! LOL!

CHAPTER 1

Nadia knew she shouldn't have been snooping around Jonathan's house, but she shrugged her conscience off with the thought that if he didn't want her looking through his stuff, he shouldn't have asked her to walk his big ol' nasty dog for six whole weeks while he was away on business. After all, it was quite an inconvenience for her to get up a half hour earlier than she was accustomed to, get a plastic trash bag, let his dog drag her small frame around the streets of Baltimore until it chose a place to release its processed dog chow, and then have to pick it up and carry it around until she got to a trash can. It grossed her out to say the least. And honestly, Nadia could think of a whole lot of things she'd rather be doing than scooping up dog poop at six thirty in the morning and seven thirty at night . . . and for free at that!

Nadia didn't even like dogs, not even the little tiny ones that only weigh about two pounds soaking wet with bows above their ears. Why anyone in their right mind would pay good money for something that's gonna leave hair all over the furniture, bite up their shoes, slob all over stuff, poop around the house, and go crazy barking in the middle of the night was beyond her. And on top of that, a dog would never, ever wash dishes, run some nice hot bathwater, cook a good meal, give a foot rub, or at the very least take the trash out every now and then. Nadia would need to get something more out of that deal than a yucky tongue lapping in her face. And as for her thoughts of a dog being able to guard her house, she had an ADT security system for that, which suited her just fine.

"Girl, why did you even agree to walk his dog if you were going to complain about it every day?" Terryn Campbell asked, rolling her eyes and wedging her cell phone between her cheek and shoulder while she wheeled her car into the parking lot of the small law office where she worked as a paralegal.

"What do you mean why?" Nadia huffed as Jonathan's dog yanked her forward from his leash. "You know this is all a part of my plan to know the man," she reminded her best girlfriend. "I had to find an edge over all these women on the prowl out here."

"They are lucky I don't live in your neighborhood, because I would give every last one of them heifers a run for their money," Terryn snickered. "I don't care how many pairs of booty-baring shorts they put on."

The day Jonathan had moved onto Bernsdale Drive a few months back, Nadia could swear that every single woman on the block suddenly found some reason to come outside. She herself had been casually lounging on her upper deck with her cell phone, a glass of wine, her journal, and a pen writing some poetry when he pulled up behind the wheel of a U-Haul truck looking as hot and sweaty as the R & B singer Tyrese in his *Nobody Else* video. He pulled into the driveway of the townhome right across from Nadia, giving her an easy and unobstructed view of everything she needed to see to feed her interest. Folding her bottom lip into her mouth, she hid behind her shades while she dialed Terryn's number.

"You need to see what just pulled up and started unloading a truckful of furniture," she whispered although she knew she was well out of her new neighbor's hearing range.

"Who is it?" Terryn asked as she stuffed papers into a manila envelope and then into a hanging file folder of a cabinet drawer. "Is he single?"

"I'm trying to catch a glimpse of his hand now, but he won't be still."

"Where are you?"

"On my deck." Nadia eased back into her chaise just a bit, enjoying the view of him both when he came outside to get stuff off the truck *and* when he took things inside, his windows not yet covered with curtains, blinds, or any other visual barrier. It was a huge advantage for Nadia because it kept her from stooping to what she considered to be the chicken-head level, which consisted of wiggling into a pair of shorts two sizes too small and taking a sudden interest in outdoor activities. Within twenty minutes of Jonathan pulling up, women were out pulling up weeds, washing their cars, and going to the mailbox. Behind her tinted lenses Nadia rolled her eyes when she saw even forty-something Feenie emerging from her front door in a halter top and a pair of supertight Baby Phat sweatpants to jump double Dutch with a few teenage girls that on a normal day she usually cussed out for one reason or another.

"You need to see this nasty woman and what she has on," Nadia shared with Terryn, crinkling her nose in disdain, thinking Feenie looked like a hot mess.

"Who, Feenie?" Terryn asked knowingly, having already heard more than a dozen times what Nadia felt about her not so young neighbor trying to hold on to her youth.

"Who else? Girl, she out here jumping rope, talking 'bout 'do the double Dutch, do the double Dutch . . . jump in, jump out.'" If getting Jonathan's attention was what Feenie was after (and it was), she did indeed achieve her goal, as during one trip Jonathan did stop and watch for about ten seconds before he shook his head, chuckling, then went back to his work. Nadia noticed and cringed, although she was embarrassed for Feenie.

"Girl, that ain't nothing but a shame and a scandal before the heavens and the earth!" Nadia scowled.

"But if you got it, you got it. Might as well use what you got."

"I guess you got a point there." Nadia twisted her lips to one side. She wouldn't admit it to anyone, but she secretly acknowledged that Feenie did have some hot moves, spinning in circles, doing half splits, and hopping on one foot, all while making her booty pop like a video chick's.

"But I don't care what nobody say, after a certain age there're just some things a full-grown woman shouldn't do." The two women giggled like schoolgirls.

For the rest of that hot summer day, from about eleven that morning until three that afternoon, Jonathan and his greasy-looking muscles kept the women on his block entertained, while they tried not to look so obvious with their ogling. Nadia continued to sun her lightly browned sugar cookie complexion, watching Johnathan's every move and plotting a strategy to meet him . . . that is, until a large black and brown dog galloped off the back of a burgundy extended-cab Chevy Avalanche that pulled up around two thirty driven by who Nadia assumed was one of Jonathan's "boys." The dog ran right for Jonathan's arms like a lost child, excitedly barking all the way, and much to Nadia's vexation Jonathan nearly pressed his lips to that dog's mouth.

"Oh my goodness! He looked like he just kissed his dog!" she gasped into the phone.

"For real!" Terryn shrieked. "Ugh! He wouldn't have to worry about kissing me after that. I'm right around the corner; I'll be there in a few minutes to see what it is y'all are slobbering over."

"Well, I don't think he actually made contact," Nadia said, trying to convince herself more than anyone else. "Because you know—lips that canine will never touch mine," she added, semicopying a line from an episode of *The Jeffersons*. "But since I didn't really get a super close-up view, I'm just going to say he only came close . . . I think. But one thing for sure—it ain't no ring on his finger."

Nadia watched inconspicuously for the next few minutes while he frolicked around outside with his "best friend" before she rose to her feet in a bikini top and hip-hugger shorts to get the door for Terryn, who had just pulled into the driveway. As she stood, she caught Jonathan's two-and-a-half-second glance up at her, which caused her heart to skip a fraction of a beat. Nadia turned seductively and bent at the waist, giving Jonathan a bit of eye candy.

"Now, how are you going to talk about the lady down the street when you're sitting on the deck in your bra and panties?" Terryn asked, cutting her eyes to point out Nadia's hypocrisy.

"First of all, I was already on my deck doing what I was doing when he arrived. Second, I didn't purposely get dressed—or undressed—then come outside just to be seen. Then third, I ain't forty-nothing. I'm twenty-six, sexy, fine, classy, and sophisticated." Nadia propped a hand on her hip and exaggerated a twist. As she closed the door, she shot her eyes over to Jonathan's yard, where he was rolling on the ground with his dog again.

"Eww!" she commented aloud with a shudder. "Y'all can have that," she said for the neighborhood hoochies as if they were all sitting in her living room.

Even so, she found herself keeping an eye on Jonathan, as he seemed to have a certain level of mystique (not to mention the man was fine!). Every morning around seven, clad in a suit and tie, he'd pull out of his garage in a late-model silver Jag with black leather interior, cruise down to the end of the block, and make a right. And about twelve hours later, he'd come coasting back onto Bernsdale Drive, jacket now off and tie now loosened, and like a bear going into hibernation, ease into the cavern of his garage, then trigger the door to slowly lower behind him. It would be about thirty minutes later that he'd emerge from his front door with his animal buddy on a leash, stretch for a few minutes, then begin an hour-and-a-half jog, which always ended at the cluster of mailboxes on Nadia's end of the street.

It wasn't so much that Nadia had been snooping on her new neighbor, but it was easy for her to figure out his pattern. Nadia worked as a trainer for an inbound technical support call center and usually didn't leave home in the mornings until seven thirty. Generally she was back no later than five. When she was at home, she called herself working on a book of poetry that she hoped to sell to some publishing house one day, so she spent hours on end in front of her computer, transferring words from her journal, then rearranging and revising them to perfection. Of course, her computer was conveniently positioned at the window that faced east, allowing her to watch the sun come up every now and then for inspiration while she sipped on a cup of vanilla-peppermint tea. Before Jonathan came along, Nadia had never shown the discipline or patience to sit and watch the sun rise. Coincidently also east was Jonathan's house, and somehow, she'd now actually seen the sun rise at least ten times, perched at her window like a bird. Even then she still sometimes missed the sun's appearance for looking down at Jonathan's driveway, watching him back out of it and cruise down the street.

Nonetheless, now that Nadia claimed to be keeping a better eye on the beauty and wonders of nature, she suddenly noticed lots of small things in her neighborhood that she'd overlooked before, like the trio of teenage sisters sneaking boys in the house when their parents weren't home, where those kids who liked to draw and paint all over the sidewalk actually lived, and how many nights a week Feenie cooked dinner. It seemed like every other night, Feenie was wiggling her jiggle to the house right across from Nadia's with a foil-covered plate in her hand. One night after the city had a bit of a downpour and it was cool enough to open the window rather than run the air conditioner, Nadia sat in her usual spot, perfect for viewing Jonathan's house, and heard Feenie's big mouth from way across the street.

"Hey, boo! I was just thinkin' 'bout you and thought you might want somma dis lasagna!" She was dressed in a denim miniskirt with a frayed hemline and a baby tee that didn't quite meet the top of her skirt. Jonathan spoke so low, Nadia couldn't hear his response, but Feenie did go in. *Later for poetry.* Nadia started watching the clock and his front door. Feenie must have just put the plate down in the kitchen or something, Nadia concluded, because not even a minute passed before she came back out again. "All right, then," she commented. "Well, just let me know if you need anything; you know I don't mind helping out." Jonathan did a couple of nods and bobs, escorting her midway down his sidewalk, with his dog trailing beside him. *Hmmm . . . definitely couldn't go knocking on his door. Gotta try another approach.*

Nadia finally got her chance to meet him the night she'd perfectly timed her visit to the mailboxes when she knew he'd be finishing up his Tuesday evening jog. She pulled her hair back into a ponytail and slipped into a brand-new pink Nike pro sports top, a pair of yoga pants, and some running shoes to make it look like she had been to the gym or something. She had her back to him when he ran up behind her.

"How're you doing?"

"Ooh," Nadia gasped, feigning being startled. "You scared me. I'm fine, thank you." She shuffled randomly through some envelopes right there at the mailbox like it couldn't wait until she got in the house.

"Sorry about that." He inserted his key into the lock of his box.

"So, how are you liking the neighborhood so far?" Nadia had to speak a little louder than normal to make sure he could hear her over all the heavy doggy breathing and panting in the background, which made her internally roll her eyes.

"It's cool," he answered, cracking a half smile while glancing through a few envelopes. "Everybody's been pretty welcoming."

"Great." She nodded.

"I'm Jonathan, by the way." He tucked his mail under his left arm and extended his hand for a shake, which Nadia almost refused, figuring that she'd be picking up animal germs, but remembered that she had a ton of hand sanitizer in the house. Plus, she wanted to see if his hands were supple and well cared for, or hard and calloused. That tidbit of knowledge would probably come in handy at some point in the future.

"Nadia," she said. His palms were smooth and fingers strong.

"Nice to meet you, Nadia. And this is Pazzo." He lowered himself to one knee and ruffled his dog behind the ears.

Yeesh, Nadia thought in disgust. "Oh." She honestly couldn't think of anything else to say. "Well, um . . . welcome to the neighborhood," she ended, beginning to walk away.

"Hey, Nadia?"

She smirked to herself before turning to meet him. "Mmm-hmm?"

"So, do you run or something?" His eyes glanced over her outfit with a nod of his head.

The last time Nadia had run was back in middle school when it was required to take the annual physical fitness test. These days, the only running she did was to the bathroom when she really, really had to pee and had held it too long. But since she considered herself to be in pretty good shape, owned about five pairs of Nikes and New Balances combined, she figured it couldn't be that hard. "Yeah. All the time," she said, referencing her sprints to the ladies' room so she wouldn't be lying . . . not exactly.

"Well, if you're ever in need of a running partner or two," he said, gesturing his head to Pazzo, "let us know. We typically get out every night about eightish."

"Really?" she asked rhetorically as if she had no idea. "Okay. I might take you up on that."

"Sounds good."

And that's how Nadia signed up to just about kill herself.

She had let another two weeks pass before she pulled on some active wear and trotted over to Jonathan's door about ten till eight. As soon as she rang the bell, the dog began barking his head off, making Nadia cautiously step back several feet. "Get back!" she heard him order. Seconds later, Jonathan opened his door dressed in gray sweats and a black T-shirt. He looked a little stressed at first, but then his face lit up when he saw Nadia as he unlocked his storm door and opened it.

"Hey, Nadia."

"Hey. I thought I'd take you up on your offer. It's getting kinda dark out and I haven't had a chance to get my run in for the week." Nadia had her iPod strapped to her new arm jigamabob she had just purchased earlier that day, and held the earbuds in her hand. "Usually Mariah does a good job of keeping me company, but that's only during the daylight hours," she added, turning her forearm toward him so he could catch a glimpse of Mariah Carey's album cover on her iPod screen.

"Um . . ." He looked behind him momentarily as if he had company or was really busy and contemplated not being pulled away from whatever he'd been doing before Nadia had rung. "I actually wasn't going to go out tonight. Do you mind if, uh . . ." He looked behind him again, and this time Nadia tried to peep around him. *Maybe Feenie done snuck in with some fried chicken gizzards or something*, Nadia thought. From where she stood she barely saw past the front door, and didn't smell the aroma of soul food or food of any other kind wafting out to meet her nose.

"Don't worry about it," she dismissed, taking a step or two backward. "Maybe another time." She wasn't about to beg him to go with her.

"Well, you know what? I'll go. Just give me a couple of minutes to get my shoes on."

"You sure?" Nadia asked, trying to show indifference.

"Yeah . . . yeah. Listen, um . . . why don't you come in for a few while I wrap a couple of things up and get my shoes?"

She paused a half second so as not to look overly anxious. "Sure." *I'm in, I'm in*, she sang in her head. *Oh, I could get to like it over here. It's nice! I could put my . . . oh Lawd, here come Bingo!* No sooner had she stepped both feet in the door than Jonathan's dog leapt to his feet and started growling.

"Be quiet," Jonathan said sternly. "Go'n and sit down." The dog didn't move at first, but at Jonathan's next statement, which was, "Did you hear what I said?" he wasted no time in obediently settling himself in a corner, and resting his head on his paws but keeping his eyes on Nadia. "You can sit right there." Jonathan nodded his head toward a mocha-brown supple leather sectional. He saw her hesitancy as she cut her eyes back and forth between him and his pet. "He won't bother you," he said assuredly.

"I hope you got insurance, because I'll sue if I

get hurt in here," she started teasingly as she fit as much of her size-10 behind into the crevice of the couch as she could. "We'll be standing right in front of Judge Judy." Jonathan chuckled and disappeared upstairs.

His few minutes turned into fifteen, which allowed Nadia to take a full visual tour of his living room, which was impeccably clean . . . and there wasn't even the slightest scent of an animal. She let her eyes roam around the unique and exquisite furnishings and accessories that sat on Jonathan's tables, adorned his walls, and framed his fireplace. She probably would have walked around a bit if the place wasn't so guarded. The one time that she did move just to cross her legs, in a split second Pazzo's head popped up like a jack-in-the-box, daring Nadia to make another move. She didn't know whether he was bluffing or not, but she wasn't willing to test it out.

"All right, I'm ready." Jonathan bounded down the stairs, reached into his front closet, and pulled out a leash. "Come on," he commanded, and immediately Pazzo ran over huffing and puffing as if it had been two days since he'd last seen his master. "Ready?" he asked, turning to Nadia.

"Sure am!" Or so she thought. They did a short stretching routine on his driveway, then started off in a slow trot. Nadia hadn't even made it to the end of the block before she was trying to hide her wheezing and gasping.

"So, Nadia, what do you do?" he asked in one smooth and easy breath.

"I work in management development," she managed to pant out, feeling her throat and chest beginning to burn. *Lawd, have mercy on me! Why did I do this?*

"Wow! Helping to build our future leaders, huh?"

"Yeah," she puffed. "How 'bout"—*gasp*—"you?"

"I'm a director of a global manufacturing company."

"Oh," she said. *Whatever that is.* "So what exactly does that mean?"

In one smooth breath he answered. "Well, in a nutshell I manage global multisite operations, optimizing capacity, execution, delivery, and costs to drive significant performance improvement. I implement and drive global sales and execute strategies to impact and assist with the design of critical metrics like quality, throughput, assets, and operating expenses."

Nadia didn't really know what he'd just said, but it impressed her just the same, and judging from the décor of his home, and the car he drove, she reasoned that his job paid him very well.

By the time Nadia, Jonathan, and Pazzo got back to their street, Nadia's feet were killing her and she felt as close to death as a generally healthy person could feel, but she'd learned that Jonathan was single, no kids—not human ones anyway, because he counted that wolfy dog of his as a son. He was thirty-four and had been at his job for eight years now. He was the only boy out of four kids total, his mom lived in Missouri, while his dad had passed away when he was six years old. He poured his heart and soul into his work, but went home to St. Louis to see his mom whenever the opportunity afforded, and he was currently working on launching a new project in Dubai.

There were some things Nadia wanted to share with him about herself, but didn't have the breath to do it. So, pretty much all he learned about her was she couldn't outrun a 1950 zombie that'd been wrapped head to toe in a sheet and moving in slow motion. It took a week and a half of soaking every night in Epsom salt for Nadia to recover. But after that, she, Jonathan, and Pazzo went running about two to three nights a week.

They were in their fourth week of trotting together (and had even started grabbing a light snack midway in the course) and getting to know each other fairly well when Jonathan popped the question.

"Nadia, I need a really big favor," he started.

Nadia had gotten much better with her breathing, talking, and jogging synchronization and was able to answer him. "Sure, what is it?"

"Remember how I told you I was working on a project in Dubai?"

"Mmm-hmm."

"Well, I have to go there on the seventeenth of next month and I'm scheduled to be there for six weeks."

"Okay?" Nadia said, urging him to continue.

"Well, if it's not too much to ask, can you see after Pazzo for me? You know, make sure he eats, walk him . . . that kind of thing."

What? Watch your John Brown dog? "Um . . ."

"It's okay if you can't do it; he just despises the kennel and I think he's gotten pretty used to seeing you now. If it's too much, I understand," he said, giving Nadia an out that she didn't take.

"No, no. I'll take care of him for you," she

agreed, kicking herself even as the words crossed the threshold of her mouth and flew into the air. *What did I say that for?*

"You sure you don't mind?" In other words, out number two that, again, Nadia didn't take.

"I got you," she promised. "As long as you leave me some instructions."

"Of course." He grinned. "I mean, Pazzo's pretty simple, but I'll write everything down and post it on the fridge."

"How am I going to get to him every day?"

"I'll leave you a key. He should be comfortable enough with you now that he won't spazz out if you come in by yourself, but I tell you what, I'll give you a key when we get back and we can start getting him used to seeing you come in the door by yourself to make sure he's okay with it."

"Yeah, let's do that because I'm highly uncomfortable with the thought of a one-hundred-pound dog spazzing out on me." As a matter of fact, Nadia was highly uncomfortable being around his dog when he was perfectly still, quiet, and slouched in his corner! She probably should have said as much, but didn't.

As agreed, he gave Nadia a key that night, and started having her let herself in. Initially Jonathan would stand right on the other side of the door waiting for Nadia to enter and instructing Pazzo to get back, but he gradually distanced himself until Pazzo saw only Nadia coming in. By the time Jonathan's trip came around, Pazzo barely moved when she entered.

So Jonathan had been gone for about three weeks, and every day, Nadia was forced to collect

Pazzo's poop, along with Jonathan's newspapers, UPS and FedEx packages, and mail. His kitchen counter was becoming pretty full, which was where she'd been stacking the envelopes addressed to him. And there it was, lying on the counter as plain as day, overlooked at least twenty-one times before . . . Jonathan's pay stub in an envelope with the seal already broken.

Now, how could she resist?

CHAPTER 2

Feenie glanced out of her bathroom window just in time to see Nadia trot down the street with Jonathan's dog for what seemed like the hundredth time. *I'ma have to watch that fast-tailed heifer down the street. She think she slick running up and down the road with my boo and his dog, but I'ma fix all that. She might be younger than me, but she too stupid to know how to cook a man a decent meal. And I know she don't know how to work her jelly like I know how to work mine.*

Still naked from her shower, she smoothed the baby oil she'd pooled into her palms on her skin, then stood in front of her full-length mirror taking inventory of her forty-three-year-old body. Her hands circled her perfectly round breasts, both firm and lifted thanks to cosmetic surgery courtesy of Medicaid. What were once size-42 double Ds causing a tremendous strain on her size-6 frame had been suctioned down to perky 34-Ds. And despite having a set of twins just eight years prior, Feenie's stomach was flat and as smooth and unmarked as a baby's bottom. As she turned slowly, she frowned at the small rounded dents in her hips and behind. "Shucks, if Jonathan cain't see past that, he ain't no real man no way." She turned back to face forward, frowned again, reminded that she'd missed her Brazilian wax appointment, then reached for her robe and exited the bathroom.

"Mia, bring me my phone," she hollered down the stairwell to one of her twins.

"Why she always call me to do stuff? She don't never call you, Cara," the eight-year-old child huffed under her breath, making sure her mother wouldn't hear her attitude. She trod up the steps and then into her mother's bedroom.

"Whatchy'all doing down there?"

"Watchin' TV."

"What's on?"

"Nine-oh-two-one-oh."

"I told y'all don't be watchin' that mess," Feenie reprimanded her, disapproving of the show's sexual innuendos.

"I told Cara that she needed to change the channel, but she left it there anyway," Mia explained.

"It better be off by the time I get down there. Now get out of here and shut my door," Feenie warned as she thumbed through the list of numbers programmed in her phone until she got to Luna's Day Spa in Ellicott City. "Is Amber there? I need an appointment."

"I can take care of that for you, ma'am. When would you like to come in?"

In a matter of minutes, Feenie had an appointment for later that day to have hair stripped from her intimate area, have hair glued to her lash line, and then have hair threaded from her eyebrows, totaling a bill of more than three hundred dollars.

Feeling a sense of rejuvenation at just the thought of her grooming session, Feenie shook off her robe, flicked on her Bose iPod player, and circled the dial until she got to her new favorite song, Flo Rida and T-Pain's "Low." Singing along with the chorus, she eased herself into a stooping position, shaking her rump on the way down. "Feenie girl, you still got it!" she said out loud in laughter. "Now all you gotta do is make him want it," she said, thinking about Jonathan. "I'ma whip it on that man!" she promised herself, circling her hips and snapping her fingers.

"Mommy, did you call me?" Cara asked from the other side of the door.

"You know good and doggone well ain't nobody said your name and you better have changed that channel downstairs."

"We did. Can we have some cookies?"

"Yeah, go 'head," she responded as she slipped into a black thong and then into a short black knit Roca Wear dress that fit her body like a glove. She grinned at the way her breasts no longer required the additional support of a bra as she spun in front of the mirror before fiddling with the ankle straps of a pair of four-inch red platform stilettos. Like a woman half her age, she sprinted down the steps and grabbed her keys and purse, getting the attention of her girls.

"What's the rules?" she barked, planting a hand firmly on her hips.

"Don't open the door for nobody; don't answer the phone if it's not your number, and don't use the stove," they answered in unison, barely looking up from the television.

"All right. I'll be back. One of y'all come lock this door." With a quick slam, and hearing the twist of the dead bolt, Feenie walked to her 2005 Eddie Bauer Edition Explorer, purchased through Liberty Ford of Baltimore's bad credit program. Upon cranking it up, music blasted from the speakers and out of the truck's lowered windows as she backed out of her driveway and zoomed down the street.

"She gone!" Cara announced, having stood at the window peeking through a tiny slit in the blinds. Right away the two girls bounded up the stairs and into their mother's bedroom, knowing that she wouldn't be back home for at least two hours. Mia started at the dresser drawer that housed Feenie's makeup, while Cara strutted to the closet to play with wigs, picking up a short spiky one first. She pulled it down over two thick long braids, then tucked the braids up, toward the back of her head. "I'ma cut my hair like this when I get fifteen."

"Mommy's not gonna let you cut your hair; she always says our hair too pretty to cut." Mia giggled, twirling her fingers around a wavy mass of locks that had loosened from the braid Feenie had put there that morning. "Here, fix this."

Cara took the hair into her hands and weaved the strands together again.

"I'm never cutting my hair. I don't want that short nappy mess like Mommy got."

"I know. She need to get that mess done." Rather than the short coarse hair that Feenie had, or the thinning straight hair of their Caucasian father, Rance, the twins had a mixture of the two grades, which was a shiny, naturally wavy head full of waist-length tresses. "I'm still gonna cut mine, but I ain't gonna let it get all balled up like that. I'ma perm it." Finishing off her sister's plait, Cara patted at the wig that still sat crooked and lumpy on her own head. "I'ma go to the club just like Mama do, and be like this." She switched on the TV to BET's *106 and Park* just in time for Lil' Wayne's "Lollipop." As the artist sang, she did a series of suggestive twists and gyrations like she'd seen Feenie do several times before.

"You nasty!" Mia giggled, watching her sister flutter her knees back and forth while circling her hips.

"Hold on." Cara suddenly stopped, then went to Feenie's nightstand and pulled out a loose cigarette. She carefully positioned it between her two fingers and pretended to take a puff before continuing her dance.

"Oooooo," Mia squealed although her eyes gleamed with excitement. "You gone get it!"

"No, I ain't. I always do this. I just make sure I put stuff back."

"Let me see it." Mia raked the various tubes of gloss and compacts back into the appropriate drawer, closed it, then dashed toward Cara. Like her sister did before her, she posed the cigarette between her fingers, then planted a hand on her hip and mocked her mother, going to the top of the staircase. "Whatchy'all doing down there?" She paused for a few seconds. "You better stop it 'fore I come down there!"

"No, wait, let me do it!" Cara ran for the closet first, got a pair of Feenie's Baby Phat pumps, and almost expertly walked over to Mia, perching the cigarette between her lips and putting a hand on her hip. "When I come down there, them dishes better be washed!" she mumbled, trying to keep the smoking stick between her lips but failing. Both girls laughed as it tumbled down the stairs followed my Mia's chasing.

"You look stupid with that wig on," Mia commented, climbing the steps in laughter.

"That's how Mommy be looking when she wear it." Cara snatched the wig off and stepped out of the pumps. "We better put this stuff back before she gets back home."

"Yeah, plus I'm hungry. Let's go make some sandwiches or something." The girls checked behind themselves to make sure they'd left nothing out of place, then galloped down the stairs to the kitchen.

Completely relaxed, brows and lashes already done, Feenie lay back and cocked her legs open, allowing the waxing attendee access to do her work. After a couple of wax applications, tugs, tweezer pulls, and a cool soothing lotion, Feenie jumped up and headed for Columbia Mall to do some shopping. On the way, she pulled out her cell to call and check on the girls.

"Hey, Mommy," Cara answered.

"Hey. Whatchy'all doing?"

"Nothing. Just watching TV."

"What's on?"

"Cartoons."

"Oh. Y'all eat?"

"Yes. We had a peanut butter and jelly sandwich and a banana and some milk."

"Mmm-hmm. Anybody call there?"

"Yes, Daddy called."

"Did y'all answer the phone?" Feenie didn't mind the girls talking to their dad as long as she was home and often gave them permission to call when they wanted to, but when she would leave them home alone, it panicked her to think that the girls might share that bit of information.

"No," Cara lied. They had actually both talked to Rance for thirty minutes apiece.

"Good. Y'all can call him when I get there."

"Okay," Cara responded with little enthusiasm, having already spoken with her daddy.

"All right. I'll be there in a little bit." Sliding her phone closed, Feenie wondered what Rance could have been calling about and why he had not called her cell. Typically, he waited for the girls to call him where the number would come up private to keep his wife Laiken's ability to trace calls difficult. "Probably hot about that child support increase I slapped on his behind," she mumbled aloud. She made a mental note to call him later.

Ten years earlier

"I need a good divorce attorney. Is you one?" Feenie asked, barging into the small law office, catching Rance Alexander completely by surprise.

"Uh, yes, ma'am, we do handle divorce cases here," Rance answered, peering over the top of his squared rimless spectacles at the fireball of a woman standing before him. "Do you need a consultation?"

"I need whatever it's gonna take to get this man out of my life," Feenie said, rolling her eyes to the ceiling. "What do I gotta do?"

"Well, first . . ." Rance glanced across his receptionist's desk for a blank client profile sheet, lifting several folders and other documents before he found a clipboard holding the forms. "I'll need you to fill this out." He handed Feenie the clipboard and an ink pen. "And I need to let you know that there's a fifty-dollar consultation fee, which will apply to your fee should you decide to retain me."

"Fifty dollars! Most lawyers don't charge you nothing just to talk to 'em for a few minutes."

"I understand, ma'am, but that's the policy of this office."

Feenie stared for a few seconds, quickly sizing Rance up. He appeared to be in his mid-forties, and favored George Clooney with dark hair, just beginning to gray at the temples. His shirt was stiff with dry cleaner's starch, although he had the sleeves rolled up as if he'd been digging through cases all day. Conservative, yet stylish, cuffed black slacks covered his lower half, along with a black leather belt circling his trim waist. "Lemme see your shoes," Feenie demanded, believing that she could tell a lot about a man judging by the shoes he wore.

"Excuse me?" Rance replied, caught off guard by her brazenness and her odd request.

"Just come from around the desk," she ordered. With a crinkled brow, he obeyed, offering a handshake as he did so.

"I'm Rance Alexander, by the way."

Feenie took his hand while her eyes shot downward to his feet. "Jerrafine Trotter-Temple, soon to be just Jerrafine Trotter." She smiled inwardly when she saw the tightly laced and tied black Cole Haans. *Oh, he know what he doing,* she assessed.

"All right, I'll pay the fifty dollars." She gave him a toothy grin that made him again crinkle his brow, but he kept his thoughts to himself. "Just give me a few minutes to do my paperwork right quick."

"Sure. My receptionist is out to lunch right now, so I'll be back to personally check on you in a few minutes."

While Feenie jotted down her basic information, she couldn't help but think about her estranged husband, Marvin Temple, and how anxious she was to get rid of him.

CHAPTER 3

Marvin and Feenie had started dating back in high school, once Feenie, a popular and snobby cheerleader, had caught wind that Marvin was being scouted by the NBA. While she never took a sincere interest in Marvin, the hopes of him having a future as a professional basketball player had been the basis of her affection and the motivation she needed to do back flips and cartwheels and chant his name and jersey number from side court. She'd spent her entire senior year fantasizing of being an NBA wife, living in a huge mansion of a home with three kids and a dog, and being shown on TV sitting in the stands at Marvin's home games. Her elation could not be described the night Marvin found out that he was being drafted. He'd run the three miles from his house to hers, and swung her off her feet the second she opened the front door to her mother's apartment.

"We're rich! We're rich!" he yelled, spinning her in circles. "I made it in, baby!"

Feenie shrieked with selfish joy as she planted

kisses all over Marvin's face. "I knew you could do it, baby! I knew it!"

"I love you, Feenie," Marvin whispered before pressing passionately into her lips.

"I love you too," she whispered back, and now with the reality of what once had been just the hopes of dollar bills at her fingertips, Feenie actually believed her own lie.

Feenie and Marvin barely had their diplomas in their hands before they headed down to the city's clerk of courts office for a marriage license. Six weeks before his appointment to sign off on a multimillion-dollar contract, Marvin took Jerrafine Trotter as his wife. They opted for a small ceremony in Marvin's parents' backyard, with plans to have a super shindig once the money starting rolling in. Feenie wore a homemade dress made of no more than a yard of fabric, most of it spent semicovering her more than ample bosom and too little of it covering her behind. A heap of multicolored weave was stacked on her head in crisp loops that intertwined with each other, and an asymmetrical bang that shielded more than half her face. Her height was elevated a full four inches by a pair of white stilettos with thin straps that wrapped from her ankles to her knees, and she carried a half dozen pink roses whose edges were beginning to brown slightly, their stems wrapped in a strip of the leftover fabric of the barely there dress. Marvin's mother hid her disdain while Feenie's mother gasped as she held her chest and patted her eyes. "Look at my baby girl! She's so beautiful!"

After he kissed his bride, the group of thirty or

so family members feasted on fried chicken, potato salad, green beans, and buttered rolls— all prepared by Feenie's mom—and a sheet cake purchased from the local grocery store bakery. Feenie and Marvin had rented a limo to transport them to a nearby hotel, where they consummated their relationship with no form of birth control. Feenie's world was crushed to bits when just a few days later, Marvin was playing on the court with some friends, took a nasty fall, and had his ankle smashed as another player inadvertently came crashing down on it after a hanging dunk. The doctors were quick to make their assessment that Marvin's ankle would never become strong enough to endure the demands that a professional basketball career would require.

Marvin looked for the unconditional love and support he'd expected from his new bride, but found that she was hardly interested in him since his fortune had been snatched away. He was devastated as he realized that everything that he thought he knew about the character and personality of his wife had been a lie. He needed her to love and support him, to comfort him, and to help him discover other areas where he could be successful and support both of them. What he got instead was a wife who refused to wait on him despite his injury, forcing him to hobble around on crutches around their small apartment, a flurry of curse words just about every time Feenie looked his way, and a pair of locked legs, though she swore that she'd never hold sex back from her man and thereby allow another woman to take her place.

Even so, he loved Feenie and wanted the

marriage to work, and told her as much with each passing day. "We won't be millionaires, but we can still make it, Feenie. I mean, we both love each other, and that's all we need to make this thing work. Forget about the money. We don't have to be rich to live; we both have jobs and make enough together to pay the rent and eat. I can work two or three jobs once my ankle heals." Most days, the only response she'd give was the rolling of her eyes. If she did open her mouth, Marvin would always regret that he'd encouraged her to speak at all.

When Feenie was alone, she would cry for hours at a time, despising her situation, and wishing she'd at least waited until Marvin began cashing checks written by the National Basketball Association before she'd upped and tied the knot. She bawled even more profusely when she realized she was pregnant by a man who had suddenly been reduced to working part-time at 7-Eleven.

And one day, while Marvin was gone to a follow-up doctor's appointment, Feenie stole away to the women's clinic, returning home a couple of hours later with an empty womb, Marvin never being the wiser that there had ever been a baby to speak of.

It was a few weeks later during a heated argument over the lack of money that Feenie saw her opportunity to blurt out words that cut Marvin like a double-edged sword.

"Babe, I'm just saying, if you go full-time instead of part-time, we could make a little bit of extra money," he said. "It's supposed to be you and me against the world, baby. We supposed to be in it together."

"See, that's where you're wrong," she replied nonchalantly as she sat on her feet nestled in the corner of the couch painting her fingernails. "What it is supposed to be is you bringing home the bacon and taking care of me, not me breaking my back slaving my life away waitin' tables to help you pay bills. It supposed to be me being able to shop wherever I want to, not me looking at the clearance rack at Target."

"I thought when we got married it was for better or for worse. That is what I heard you say before the minister, your mama, my mama, and the Lord."

Feenie sucked her teeth. "Don't nobody mean that mess. And you crazy in your head if you think I'ma sit here and baby you and pat you up when you supposed to be a man. And a real man takes care of his woman."

"So, what are you trying to say, Feenie? I'm not a real man just because I broke my ankle? Just because I'm asking my wife to help me like a wife is supposed to do?"

"I ain't supposed to do jack smack, but give you somma dis right here," she snapped, jerking her legs open and pointing to her crotch. "And I can tell you right now, I ain't free and I ain't cheap! And if you think I'ma keep on wasting my good stuff on you, you best think again! What I got is gold, and truth be told, I supposed to be married to and givin' it up to a millionaire, not to some broke-tailed, jack-leg, tryna-make-a-dollar-outta-fifteen cents, cain't-half-pay-the-bills joker like you!"

Marvin was initially stunned as he watched

Feenie bring her knees together and begin attending to her fingernails again. His hands balled into tight angry knobs as for the first time he recognized Feenie for what she really was. "You ain't nothin' but a materialistic, gold-diggin', ghetto ho!"

Like an attacking tiger, Feenie leapt to her feet in lightning speed, made a near-twelve-inch reach to Marvin's face, and slapped him so hard his head did a quarter turn. In an instant and without thinking, he retaliated by shoving her in the face, so that she stumbled backward over the coffee table. She landed on her butt, but her right arm slammed against the table's edge, while her head landed into the cushion of the couch. Shrieking out in pain, Feenie scrambled to her feet grabbing her arm, then fell to the floor crying hysterically.

"I'm sorry, baby; I'm sorry," Marvin said, remorsefully falling to his knees. He tried to take her in his arms, but Feenie was having none of it.

"Get away from me!" she cried, jerking at his touch.

"Feenie, please. I didn't mean that."

"Yes, you did!" She looked up into her husband's face and saw her chance to completely manipulate the situation. Feenie suddenly moved her hand from her arm to her belly. "Oww!"

Marvin's look changed from remorse to confusion. "What? What is it?" He leaned to reach out a second time to his wife.

"Get away from me, Marvin!" She dug her feet into the carpet, wildly scooting away from him like a wounded and terrified animal. Leaning against the sofa, Feenie began panting heavily as she let her tears flow.

"What is wrong?" Marvin asked again, becoming panicked. Feenie sat silent for close to two minutes, while tears seeped through her closed lids. Not knowing what else to do, Marvin sat beside her wishing he could undo the mess he'd created. Cautiously, while Feenie's eyes were still shut, he reached up and stroked her hair. This time Feenie didn't pull away.

"Gimme my purse," she said between sobs. Without question, Marvin moved at her command, went to their bedroom, and came back with a large faux Coach bag she'd received as a graduation gift. Still sobbing, she dug around in the bag for a few seconds until she pulled out a folded sheet of paper, then handed it to her husband. "I was going to wait until our three-month anniversary to tell you," she whispered.

Marvin unfolded the paper and glanced over the writing that confirmed Feenie's positive pregnancy test. "You're pregnant?" he asked gently as his eyes watered with tears. Feenie nodded, although she knew their baby had long been gone. Marvin rested his hand on her stomach, buried his head into her chest, and cried for the next several minutes. As best he could, he leapt to his feet. "Come on, we need to take you to the emergency room."

"But we don't have insurance, babe."

"That doesn't matter. Come on." He helped Feenie to her feet, beside himself with guilt as he watched her nurse her arm. Gulping back tears, he led her to the car and sped to the nearest hospital.

Once Feenie told the intake nurse that she thought her baby's life was at stake, it was only minutes before she and Marvin were taken to an examination room.

"Mrs. Temple," a female doctor greeted, coming into the room. "How are you feeling?"

"I don't know," Feenie whined. Marvin held his head down staring at the tiles in the floor.

"I fell in my living room and hit my arm on the table," she answered, knowing it was more important for her scheme to protect her husband by not divulging the entire truth.

"And you're expecting, is that right?"

"Yes, ma'am."

"How far along are you?"

"About nine weeks," she lied.

"And who's your doctor?"

"I haven't picked one yet."

"You know prenatal care is very important to your baby's health," the doctor said in a gentle reprimand.

"Yes, ma'am."

"I'ma make sure she gets the best care out there," Marvin added.

"We'll need to X-ray your arm, but first let me listen for the baby's heartbeat," the doctor stated, reaching first for her stethoscope. She laid the cold device against Feenie's belly as her eyes stared intently at nothing in particular. Her brows crinkled as she circled the tool on Feenie's skin. "The baby may be in trouble; I'm not hearing a heartbeat."

Marvin's heart stopped while Feenie turned on a new flood of tears. A few seconds later, though still listening and searching, the doctor turned her lips inwardly and slowly shook her head. "We'll run some tests to be more conclusive, but I'm not hearing anything. I'll be right back."

"My baby!" Feenie began shrieking. "My baby!" Once the doctor left the room, Feenie looked at Marvin and began screaming out every foul name in the book, cursing him up one side and down the other. "Get out! Get out now, Marvin! I hate you and I don't ever wanna see you again!"

Marvin uttered his apologies over and over again, trying to calm his wife down by wrapping his arms around her, but the more he tried, the more Feenie flailed her arms. "Get the hell outta my room!"

Not wanting the commotion to continue, Marvin tucked his tail and left quietly. He sat in the parking lot for the next two hours crying and wondering how his life had taken such an awful turn. Instead of the basketball star he'd almost become, he concluded that Feenie was right. All he was was a broke, minimum-wage-earning, no-insurance-having black man with no plans for a future. And now he'd killed his own child.

From that day on, no matter what she did, in Marvin's eyes Feenie could do no wrong . . . and she knew it.

CHAPTER 4

After Nadia saw Jonathan's check stub that day, she just couldn't stop herself from looking at other things. She felt that she had honestly tried to, but every day something new would catch her attention. A couple of days ago, it was his mail. With a quick glance inside his Baltimore Gas and Electric envelope she found out that his electric bill was significantly lower than hers this month. How did he manage that? His cell phone bill was crazy high, though, and he must have loved to shop at Sam's Club because he had a few of their sales circulars stacked on the corner of the kitchen table. There was an American Express envelope on the table too, but it hadn't yet been opened, so Nadia left it alone and let herself out.

The next day, the brass knobs affixed to the cherry wood cabinetry called out to her. Easy as pie, she slid a drawer open, peeking inside. His cutlery lay neatly in the drawer, all stacked together in their designated spots, not scattered all over the place like hers. All of his dishes matched, and he even had a full set of matching cast-iron cookware. She pulled out the griddle and pretended to be flipping flapjacks for breakfast, shaking the flattened pan, then jerking it upward.

"Babe! Your food is almost ready!" Nadia said out loud in a mock yell upstairs. Instead of Jonathan trotting down to the kitchen, Pazzo came over wiggling his nose like he could almost smell pancakes, but then went back to his usual spot in the living room corner. Nadia put the griddle back, then peeked in the little drawer of the stove right beneath the oven. A muffin pan sat on top of a broiler pan—both were squeaky clean. It was easy to imagine Jonathan with a broiler pan, but a muffin pan? Jonathan made muffins? She giggled at the thought.

Today, Nadia was curious about what was in the pantry closet and other closets on the lower level of his home. Pazzo was running around in circles, ready to get outside, but Nadia put off taking him out for a few minutes while she went forward with what was turning out to be her daily exploration session. Each day, Nadia felt less guilty about eyeing his things, so what once might have taken a few minutes of contemplation now only took a split second of decision making. Just as if she lived there, she headed to the kitchen and swung the pantry door open to find it was filled with name-brand foods and was arranged neat as a pin, all labels facing forward as if that deranged husband from *Sleeping with the Enemy* were his roommate. There were rows and rows of canned goods ranging from sliced peaches to sliced beets to stewed tomatoes to seasoned collard greens. There were even a few cans of Spam neatly arranged in the "meat" section, along with tuna, chicken, Vienna sausages, and potted meat. *Bleck!* The box section featured a full line of Betty Crocker products and Uncle Ben rice varieties. There was even a full case of fifty-five-dollar-a-bottle Bling H20. Nadia picked up a bottle and admired the handcrafted Swarovski crystals, but nearly dropped it when the doorbell rang, startling her. Right away, Pazzo darted for the door barking all the way while she tiptoed toward it slowly, then leaned toward the peephole. It was Feenie, whorishly dressed and holding a pan of something. For a few seconds Nadia's mind bounced back and forth between whether she should open the door or not. From out of nowhere, Nadia got the idea to run upstairs and look for Jonathan's robe to throw on over her clothes. Though she didn't know if he even had one, she didn't let that deter her from charging up the stairs. Because Jonathan's house was just like her own, she didn't have to guess where the master bedroom was—and luckily, Jonathan had left his robe hanging on the edge of the bathroom door in the hallway. Nadia wasted no time stripping out of a pair of sweats and a T-shirt and her bra while hollering down the stairwell, "Just a minute!" Nadia bent over at the waist, hanging her head upside down, and ruffled her fingers through her hair to make it look disheveled. In a flash she bounded down the stairs, then cracked the door.

"Yes?" Nadia asked in her most sultry voice,

pleased at the taken-aback expression on Feenie's face.

"Where Jonathan at?" Feenie demanded, trying to see past Nadia.

"He's busy." She shrugged nonchalantly.

"Well, I need to see him, because he told me to bring this dinner over here," she quickly fabricated.

"Oh, I'll take it to him." Nadia casually put forth her hand to accept the casserole dish from Feenie.

"Uh-uh. I got this. Jonathan!" she yelled, trying to step a foot inside the door. "Jonathan, I'm here with your dinner."

Nadia let the robe gape open for a flash of a second, baring her breasts. "Woops!" Nadia chuckled, quickly closing the robe and leaning against the door frame. "I told you he's busy, but I'll be glad to take this to him."

"You gone let me get up in here! I will give it to him myself!" Feenie pushed against the door, trying to force her way inside, but instantly stopped when Nadia called out, "Pazzo!"

Upon her call, Pazzo rushed down the stairs and to the front door barking, making Feenie retract her steps. "Now, if you don't want me to sic this dog on you, you're either going to leave with that plate or leave without it. But you *are* going to leave," Nadia said matter-of-factly.

Feenie rolled her eyes as she turned away. "I'll be back," she promised.

"I'll be here," Nadia answered smugly, then closed the door and laughed out loud as she journeyed back upstairs to return the robe and see what she could find. As soon as she reached the top of the staircase, a terrible odor hit her nose. She took the robe off, sniffing the air with every step, hung the robe back in the place she'd pulled it down from, then followed her nose to Jonathan's bedroom, pushing the door open slowly.

"Oh . . . my . . . goodness!" Nadia stood in the doorway and gasped.

Instead of being so concerned about what kind of dishes and food Jonathan had, Nadia realized that she should have been doing what he'd asked her to do, and that was to take his stupid dog outside. Pazzo apparently couldn't hold back his bowels and had left a huge pile of poop right in front of the master bathroom door. Her hand flew to her nose and mouth to fight the smell and hold back the urge to puke. Not yet ready to attack the disaster, Nadia shut the bedroom door, then sat on the steps thinking and contemplating about leaving that mess there until Jonathan returned in another two weeks. *I could easily pretend that I didn't know anything about it. I mean, Pazzo could have gotten sick during the day while I was at work and had no way to get out. Which was really what had happened. Well, not the sick part, but the part about not being able to get out,* she reasoned mentally.

The only thing about that was once during one of Nadia and Jonathan's jogs, she'd asked several dog-related questions, and Jonathan had shared that Pazzo had never had an accident in the house since he'd been housebroken, and he had had this dog for about five years now. Nadia was pretty certain that he wouldn't buy that all of a sudden an accident had happened. With an exaggerated sigh, she heaved herself up from the steps, went to the lower level, and began looking for cleaning supplies. Which was a pretty darn good reason for her to search through just about every single cabinet in the house. Jonathan kept his house pretty immaculate, and had all kinds of Lysol, Pine-Sol, Carpet Fresh, Kaboom, Kapow, Kabam, Bang, Badda-Bing, and everything else.

It took her the better part of an hour to clean up behind Pazzo and scrub the carpet. When she finished, the carpet was soaked and distressed looking, but the bedroom smelled superduper clean. Well, actually it smelled superduper chemically.

When she was finally done, Nadia did take Pazzo out anyway, just in case he had some unfinished business. Well, she didn't really take him *out* out. It was too late and dark for her to go running around the city, so she just let him run around in the backyard for about thirty minutes.

And while he did that, Nadia busied herself by going back to Jonathan's bedroom to take a look at a few things that had caught her eye. His bed looked like it belonged in a hotel, simplistic and clean. There was a huge oak headboard with intricate carvings that was affixed to the wall; then on the bed were several down pillows in white cases, along with pristine white linens over a feather bed thingy. Lying across the foot of the bed was a royal-blue duvet neatly folded and hanging over the sides. It was very inviting, but Nadia resisted . . . at least this particular time. A fifty-two-inch flat-screen TV was positioned on the wall opposite the bed, with the dresser right below.

Atop the dresser was a nifty little oak box with a glass top that held about ten wristwatches; there was some other kind of box that held cuff links and necktie clip things, and another that held Jonathan's loose change. As if there were someone home who would hear her moving around, Nadia quietly slid a drawer open to find several pairs of socks neatly folded together; there were T-shirts in the next, and boxer briefs in the one below that.

She peeked into a few more drawers but found nothing exciting.

Satisfied with her search for the day, Nadia called Pazzo back into the house, ordered him to his corner, then locked up Jonathan's house and crossed the street to her own, once again feeling guilty and reprimanding herself for going through his stuff like she'd done before . . . and for no reason at that. But then it hit her as to what she was looking for: traces of a girlfriend, significant other, ex-wife, bed buddy, or whatever he had going on. He was too fine not to be seeing somebody. And if he was seeing somebody on some level, there was bound to be a trace of her somewhere. Even if it was nothing more than a bobby pin or a Maxi Pad wrapper.

By the time she entered her own front door, Nadia's phone indicated three new messages on her voice mail. She put the phone on speaker and let them all play.

"Nadia, I need to talk you—*tonight*! If you don't do anything else before you go to sleep, you better make it your business to call me."

Nadia could tell not just from the message but also from the clamoring of the receiver against the phone's base that her dad was beyond PO'd. The next two messages were from him too, and she was sure that the intermittent chiming of her cell phone was a further indication that if she didn't call him tonight he was going to be driving up from South Carolina to have her head on a platter. Before she called her dad, she called Terryn.

"Girl, I'm in so much trouble," she started.

"What is it that you have done now?" Terryn huffed. "You stay in trouble."

"My dad is gonna kill me!"

"He is probably so used to bailing you out month after month, it probably doesn't even faze him anymore."

"No, you don't understand. See, what had happened was, my daddy, Aidan—which is Nadia spelled backward, by the way"—she added although she'd told Terryn that one hundred times before, but always said it whenever she called out his first name—"McKenzie Mitchell let me use his MasterCard, after I called him in tears telling him that a few of my bills were behind and I needed some help with them. He was like 'How much are they, Nadia? Add them up and tell me what you need and I'll take care of it.' Now, you know I don't have any credit card debt, so I was only talking about a few things like my current car payment, my power bill, my cell phone bill, house phone, cable, Internet, water, sewage, insurance, groceries, and gas for my car, which was, like, fifteen hundred dollars when I added it all up."

"What in the world? When is the last time you paid bills, girl?" Terryn balked, although she had a tendency to pay bills late herself.

"That is the exact same thing my dad said," Nadia replied. "Anyway, I told him I had just paid bills last month with the check he'd sent me, but what I didn't tell him was that about half of that money went to that new power suit, blouse, and shoes and matching purse I picked up that time you and I went shopping."

"Mmm-hmm. See, there you go."

"But really, it was actually a necessity for my job. Since I'm always up in front of new-hire employees every day, it's always up to me to set a professional tone, and I couldn't exactly do it like I needed to in my Value City suits. Girl, you know Daddy is a professional dresser and he wears a suit ehhhhh-very day that the Lord sends. Even on Saturdays."

"Yeah, I remember Mr. Mitchell always being decked out."

"Right, so I'm thinking that surely he could support me sharpening my wardrobe up just a bit. Anyway, half that money went to Nordstrom's, but he didn't need to know all that, but then he was like, 'You couldn't have spent it all on bills,'" Nadia said, lowering her tone to give her best impersonation of her father. "I was like, 'Yes, I did, Daddy. I can send you all my receipts to show you.' Girl, I was crossing my fingers, my toes, *and* my eyes hoping he wouldn't say exactly what he said."

"Which was what—send him the receipts?" Terryn rightfully guessed.

"Yep," Nadia sighed.

"So what did you tell him?"

"What else could I tell him but 'yes, sir'? Then he asked me when I was going to send them and

I told him I would send them this Friday as soon as I get them together."

Terryn started laughing. "What are you going to do about that?"

"Pray that the Lord lets him forget all about it." Nadia couldn't help but laugh at herself. "But then he said that I better not ask him for any more money until I sent those receipts."

"And then . . . ?" Terryn asked, already knowing how the story would end. She could hear Nadia's smile through the phone lines.

"And then he gave me his card number along with the expiration date and three-digit security code and told me I bed' not run up his card."

"Girl, I wish I had a daddy like Aidan—that's Nadia spelled backward—McKenzie Mitchell! Shoot—I'd take a mama like him if a daddy wa'n't available."

"Well, right now, I'd take a no daddy over the one that's mad at me for spending too much money! I don't know how I'm going to dig myself out of this one." Nadia flopped down on her couch and clicked through television channels as she began trying to figure out how she was going to send receipts that she didn't have to her dad.

"You know what always helps me think?" Terryn offered.

"What?"

"A jumbo margarita from Holy Frijoles."

"Mmmm," Nadia moaned. "That does sound good right about now."

"If you agree to buy me at least two, I'll help you brainstorm on what to tell your daddy."

"You make me sick," Nadia balked.

"Go throw up, then. You want my help or not?"

Nadia sucked her teeth, then blurted her response. "I'll meet you there in thirty minutes." She spruced her face up a little with a coat of mascara and some tinted lip gloss, pulled on a pair of tight black pants that read "Check This Out" across her behind, and a white shelf bra cami. She pushed her feet into her new pair of FitFlops, the fifty-dollar flip-flops that were supposed to tone up her legs and buttocks, then checked her booty in the mirror to try to determine if the shoes were working. She frowned, really unable to see a difference, but then again, Nadia thought her butt looked great in the first place, so she just grabbed her keys and headed for the restaurant.

Right on time, Terryn came in dressed like the character Toni Childs from *Girlfriends*, in a silk scarf wrapped around her head Hollywood-style, and a pair of oversized shades.

"Who you tryna hide from?" Nadia poked as she slid into the seat across from her.

"Hide? Girl, all this beauty can't be hidden!" Terryn whipped away her accessories, then dug in her purse to find her Mac compact and checked her reflection. "Wooo! My mama and them did a good job making me!"

"Whatever. You are so narcissistic."

"I'm so what?" She crinkled her nose up at Nadia, in sincere ignorance.

"You don't know how to use context clues? You so deg-gone stuck on yourself, vain, conceited, bigheaded, arrogant. Need I go on? How you have a college degree and don't know what narcissistic mean?"

She sniffed at the air. "You smell that?"

Nadia looked upward as she inhaled with a puzzled look on her face. "I don't smell anything but peppers and onions."

"I do and I know that scent anywhere . . . it's . . . *hater*!" Terryn burst into giggles as if she were seriously funny.

"Anyway!" Nadia tossed her napkin at her. "I need you to help me think."

"About what?"

"What do you mean about what? Didn't we already have this conversation? Did you start drinking before you got here? I told you my dad wants me to send him the receipts from last month to show that I paid all my bills like he gave me the money to." A server interrupted to get their drink orders, and then Nadia continued. "But like I said, I didn't exactly pay my bills with the money."

"What did you do, go shopping?"

"Why are you asking me this all over again? You make me sick when you do that."

"Because that is what the attorneys do. They ask the same questions over and over to see if you gone tell the same lie, if you lying. I have to practice my attorney skills."

"Like I said—I hate when you do that."

"Because you're a hater, but I love you just the same." Terryn gave Nadia a cheesy grin, then ducked behind her menu. "What are we eating?"

"I don't know what you are going to eat, because I only promised to pay for two drinks. If you tryna get full off my tab, you need to try another strategy," Nadia replied, glancing over her own menu.

"All I can say is this, you stay in more mess."

Terryn pushed a long strand of hair behind her ear. "And you are too old to be living out of your daddy's wallet."

"That's one of the benefits to being an only child."

"So what are you gonna do?"

Nadia shrugged. "That is why I'm paying for your drinks, so you can tell me." The server came back with two jumbo glasses of colored tequila, and the ladies wasted no time bringing them to their lips.

"Well, one thing you can do is pay your bills, then send him the receipts like he asked," Terryn snorted.

"If it were that easy, we wouldn't be here." Nadia slid more of her frozen beverage down her throat. "How about this? You give me the receipts from your bills from last month—they don't have your name on them, do they?"

"Girl, I pay all my bills online automatically through my checking account, so I can't help you. Let's order an appetizer." She caught the server's eye, placed an order for some hot wings and fries and an order of quesadillas, then turned back to Nadia. "Tell him you pay your bills online so you don't have any paper receipts."

"Then he's gonna tell me to send him my bank statements so he can check them. That ain't gonna work."

"Okay, tell him that you shredded them already and you'll have to ask for duplicates, or for your next statement to release, which will show the last payment amount, but in the meantime, you need some money now."

"That just might work. I'll try it." Nadia took a break to bite into a quesadilla, then swallowed. "Consider your drinks earned." She held up her drink glass and clinked it against her friend's. "So, what's going on with you?"

"Helping this new temp girl get on the ball with her job. She just started today and don't know how to do nothing," Terryn answered. "We really did need some admin help, though—so I'm not going to complain too much."

"Sounds like fun."

"A hot mess is more like it. Girl, so many people come in and out of there with all kinds of cases it's not even funny. Do you remember Renee Turner from high school?"

"Who could forget her? Her nose was so high up in the air it practically touched the ceiling."

"Well, girl, she is on charges for assault and battery. Knocked her husband upside the head with a brick and he pressed charges."

"What?"

"Yes, ma'am. Don't tell nobody this, because you know this is all superconfidential information," Terryn interjected.

"Of course. Who would I tell anyway?"

"I'm just saying."

"Treyvon Johnson has about fifty-eleven baby mamas, and all of them trying to get that child support."

"I can't fault them for that. If he made the baby, then he needs to be the daddy. And to think that joker tried to holla at me last year."

"You did right 'cause he ain't a bit of good." Terryn updated Nadia on the personal lives of a few more people they both had known before they ended their mini girls' night out, with Nadia slapping her credit card on the table, footing the entire bill.

When Nadia got home, the excuse that Terryn helped her think of was exactly what she told her dad. And to her surprise, it worked. As soon as she hung up the phone with permission to use Aidan's card once more, she went online and paid every bill she had. Then Nadia went on eBay and bought the newest model of the Black-Berry Pearl that she'd been wanting for ages.

Nadia knew the BlackBerry wasn't a bill, but she'd used her dad's card anyway, She could already hear his tirade, and proactively worked out how the scene would play out in her mind.

"I'm trying to figure out how it is that you took it upon yourself to use my credit card for an unauthorized purchase," he would say calmly. *That would be enough to make her knees buckle; it was only when he was at his angriest that he spoke calmly, as backward as it seemed to Nadia.*

"I, um . . . I, well, I thought I mentioned it to you when you gave me the card number." He wouldn't comment. *That meant he wasn't buying it. "You didn't hear me when I asked you that?" she'd bluff.*

"Nadia, I don't know who you think you're talking to. When you called me you know you did not mention going on a shopping spree on eBay."

"Dad, I did," she'd say. *"I told you, like, two months ago that my old phone was cracked."* At that point, she would jump to her feet, scoot to her front door, and knock loudly. *"Hold on, Dad. Who is it?"* After a few seconds

she'd call out, "Hold on a sec. Dad, it's the police, I need to call you back."

"The police? For what?"

Nadia would thump on her door a second time. "I don't know, Dad. Something must have happened in the neighborhood. Let me call you back before they kick my door down."

"Make sure you do that."

"Yeah, that should work," she concluded, although she knew her dad would know full well that she'd just decided to use his card. But he was the one who'd spoiled her so bad. She sauntered into the kitchen, grabbed a package of Orville Redenbacher's extra butter, and tossed it in the microwave. Three minutes later Nadia took a seat at her computer trying to work through another poem when her new-e-mail indicator chimed. Her eyebrows shot up when she saw she had a message from Jonathan.

From: Jonathan.Strickland@Infiniteglobalindustries.com
To: Aidans1babygirl@yahoo.com
Subject: Hey, Nadia!
Hey, Nadia,
Hope all is going well in the States. How's Pazzo? I really appreciate you looking after him while I'm away. I know he can be quite a handful. I'd like to offer you a proper thank-you by taking you out to dinner when I return. You choose the place. The sky's the limit. It's the least I can do.
Take care and see you in another week,
JS

That brought a huge smile to her face and a couple of fairy-tale visions to her head. Nadia could picture the two of them cruising down the streets of D.C. in his Jag with people looking at them wondering where they were going and how much money they had. "Oh, I definitely have to find something fly to wear!" she said aloud.

From: Aidans1babygirl@yahoo.com
To: Jonathan.Strickland@Infiniteglobalindustries.com
Subject: RE: Hey, Nadia!
Hi, Jonathan,
Dinner sounds great, but I will need to check my schedule and get back to you before you get back.
Nadia

Nadia already knew she'd be free, but the busy and hard-to-get method seemed to always work out better, at least that was what Aidan had always advised her to do.

"Make a man work for you, baby. If he's really interested in you, he gone do whatever it takes. But if you give him a reward with no work, then what you telling him is you ain't worth workin' for, and he'll walk all over you everytime," he'd said. Nadia had found out through her college years that Aidan was exactly right. Every guy she'd freely given her time and/or herself to always treated her poorly and dropped her like a hot rock. Those that had to do a little work always stayed a little longer and treated her better.

Even though Nadia had given Jonathan a bit of a brush-off, right away she jetted to the closet to look for something to wear and pondered upon where she would want him to take her. Since she'd seen his check, she knew that Jonathan was definitely "paid," so she determined to pick somewhere twice as pricey as her normal hangout spots. "That way, I won't look like I come too cheap, but at the same time, I won't come off like some kind of money-hungry, pocket-digging bourgeois queen wannabe. Like Feenie!" she said with a snicker.

CHAPTER 5

Ten years earlier

"Mrs. Temple, what are the grounds for your husband's seeking a divorce?" Rance asked, lacing his fingers and placing them under his chin.

Feenie shrugged. "I 'on't know. Guess he just don't love me no more since I gained a little weight." Feenie glanced down at her narrow hips, knowing she hadn't gained a single pound since high school. "I don't understand it." The truth was Feenie knew full well why Marvin had decided to end the marriage. Not only was she mean and manipulative, but he'd caught Feenie cheating at least three times, walking into his home after working double shifts and finding his wife lying on her back spread-eagle for another man.

"What the . . ."

Cyrus Williams, a former schoolmate who was home from college where he'd gotten a full football scholarship, leapt to his feet and scrambled for his pants and a red University of Maryland sweatshirt featuring a scowling Diamondback terrapin.

"Uh . . . w'sup, Marvin?" he managed to say nervously. Cyrus's stature didn't allow him to meet Marvin eye-to-eye, but what Marvin had in height, Cyrus had in width and density. Though he'd never known Marvin to be the fighting type, he kept his eyes on him and his guard up just in case something had changed within the last year.

Marvin stood speechless in the doorway, both his spirit and his ego crushed. Feenie quickly gathered the sheet around her, tucking folds under her arms as she attempted to stutter out a few words of explanation, but nothing she said made sense. Marvin's lips tightened into a ball as he turned away, went to the living room couch, and took a seat, leaning forward and resting his elbows against his knees, numb and utterly flabbergasted. It was less than a minute later when Cyrus, silently and as inconspicuously as a 274-pound man could, jetted to and through the front door. Chewing on the insides of his mouth, Marvin fumbled with, inspected, and twisted his keys around his fingers lost in a sea of thoughts. Feenie stayed hidden in the bedroom, listening for Marvin's movement and quietly slipping into a pair of loose-fitting pajama pants and a T-shirt. Only hearing the jingling of keys, she wasn't quite sure what to think, but thought it best to stay put although she longed for a shower. Actually the moistness between her legs made her yet long for Cyrus, resenting the fact that he'd not been able to finish her off. With Cyrus in mind, but cognizant of Marvin's dawdling in the living room, she got back into bed, slid a hand into her pants, and brought herself to the point of satisfaction, then dozed off as if in a drunken stupor.

"Wake up, Feenie, we need to talk."

Feenie popped her eyes open to find Marvin looming over her, his voice stern yet gentle. A quick glance at the clock revealed to her she'd been asleep for nearly two hours.

"It's three o'clock," she mumbled, rolling her eyes back to closing. "We can talk in the morning." Just as she nestled into the pillow, pulling the covers up over her shoulder, Marvin snatched them away, catching her by surprise.

"No, we need to talk now!" he demanded.

"Or what? Or what, Marvin? You gonna fracture my arm again or kill another baby?" she spewed, snatching the covers back and repositioning herself back to comfort. "I said we'll talk later."

The words sliced through him, like they always did whenever he and Feenie had had verbal disagreements since that deceitful day. And although he'd come to expect her to spew those very words, they always affected him the same way.

He let out an exasperated sigh and sat down on the bed. "Feenie, I think we need to talk about this now. You don't think I deserve some kind of explanation?"

Beneath the covers Feenie cringed. She hated Marvin and the fact that she was married to him. The only reason why she hadn't left him was that not only could she get away with murder, but he bent over backward to please her in a futile attempt to rid himself of his overwhelming guilt. "Feenie," he called out. She answered with a soft fake snore, hoping he would shut up. "Feenie, please. Please talk to me," he begged. She snored a second time but a bit heavier. Marvin pushed a jawful of air through his lips, then shuffled back to the living room to sleep on the couch. Just before six the next morning, Feenie showered, lotioned her skin, and slipped into a brushed satin butter-yellow chemise. She padded down the hallway and to Marvin's side, where she lowered herself to her knees and forced a stream of crocodile tears down her cheeks, then leaned in to kiss her husband's cheek. He stirred a bit, then fluttered his eyes open to meet Feenie's. "Baby, I'm so sorry," she whispered. Marvin kept silent and listened. She moved forward to kiss him again, but Marvin drew back. With an exaggerated sigh, she added more words. "There's nothing I can say to fix this. I just needed something more and you wa'n't giving it to me," she said softly, putting on an act of shame.

"Why didn't you just tell me what you needed or wanted, Feenie? You know I'd give you the world."

"I didn't want to hurt your feelings."

"You don't think that hurt me? Seeing you laid up with another man? You thought that would hurt me less than just telling me what you needed?"

"You just . . ." Feenie hesitated purely for effect. "You just not big enough." Before turning her head away, she glanced at the shocked and hurt look on Marvin's face. "And you don't know how ta—"

Marvin threw his hand up. "Just stop, Feenie. You don't have to say nothing else." He shot to his feet, patted his pocket to confirm that his car keys were on his person, and headed for the front door. "I'll be back."

"I'm sorry, baby," Feenie called out behind him, but it didn't stop Marvin's motion. "Where're you going?" Her question was answered by a resounding door slam.

No sooner had he shut the door than she got on the phone and called Cyrus back, knowing he would answer regardless of the time.

"Girl, don't be getting me caught up in no mess!" he snarled, mixing in curse words.

"Don't worry about that; I got that. All you need to worry about is finishing what you started last night."

Instead of going to work that day, Feenie spent the day with Cyrus, coaxing him to spend a portion of his scholastic stipend on a short, tight minidress and a pair of stilettos that she promised to wear for him later.

Marvin called in sick for his second job, then returned home after his day-shift job with a bagful of instructional videos and books ready to work on pleasing his wife. But Feenie was gone for the weekend.

Crossing one leg seductively over the other, Feenie poured out a fabricated sob story to Rance, explaining that once Marvin realized he'd been passed over by the NBA, he became unbearable to live with. "First he started making me work more hours on my job," she started.

"Where do you work?" Rance asked, beginning to jot down a few notes.

"At the Super Laundry on St. Paul Street," she answered, glancing up just long enough to catch Rance's wandering eye. His line of vision was focused a few inches below her chin. She looked away as he quickly attempted to regain eye contact.

"How long have you been working there?"

"Almost four years now; I started when I was sixteen, working part-time, then went to full-time once I finished school. I didn't really mind working there, but then when I got pregnant, it got kinda hard because it's hot in there with them machines and stuff, so I started working part-time again and he ain't like that."

"What do you mean?"

"I mean he got mad 'cause I wa'n't making as much money no more. He started coming home cussin' me out and then he put his hands on me." Feenie lifted her arm to show off the scar from her fall on the coffee table. "I still got this mark right here. But that ain't the worst scar." She moved her hand and laid it gingerly across her belly and nearly whispered, "I cain't never get that baby back." She slid a narrow finger beneath her lower lash line, smearing away a tear before it had a chance to leave the corner of her eye.

"I'm sorry." Rance paused respectfully before continuing, reaching for and offering her a tissue. "Do you have any other children?"

Feenie shook her head and smeared away more tears. "I've not been able to get pregnant since then," she lied again; she had actually aborted one other baby without Marvin's knowledge. "Can I get alimony?"

"Well, we'll talk about that and any assets as I

begin to build your case. He's the one who has initiated the divorce, is that right?"

"Yes." Feenie nodded in her feigned state of depression. "I just never thought he'd do something like this to me."

"It'll be all right," Rance assured her, rising from his seat. "I'll start pulling some things together and have my secretary, Cathy, give you a call in about a week or so." He walked Feenie to the door and shook her hand. "You'll be hearing from me soon."

"Okay," she responded shakily. "I wanna keep the car too," she added, pulling a set of keys from the mouth of her purse.

"I'll see what I can do."

"Thank you."

Rance simply nodded, then turned to go back to his office.

Two weeks later, he chastised himself for allowing Feenie to take up so much time in his thoughts. It wasn't that he didn't have other cases to work on, but for some reason, one he couldn't quite put his finger on, why he found Feenie so attractive . . . intriguing even. Well, he could if he pondered on it, and oftentimes he found himself doing just that. He knew it was the bronzed glow of her skin highlighted by the tangerine sundress she'd worn the day she came bursting into his office. It was the teasing curvature of her breasts with just enough cleavage exposed to be inviting without being whorish. It was her tiny waistline, the way no panty line showed around her behind, the scent of vanilla musk she sprayed on her pulse points, and the way she drew attention to her already bright eyes framed with long silky lashes with a soft brown liner.

"What are you thinking about?" his wife, Laiken, asked one night as she lay in his arms after a session of lovemaking.

Rance was silent for a few seconds, but responded, "Nothing." Truth be told, he just couldn't get Feenie out of his mind.

"You were great," she commented, planting kisses on her husband's chest, then smoothed down its hairs with a few strokes of her hand. "Did you take some Viagra or something?"

Rance chuckled. "No."

"Well, what did you eat today? I need to feed it to you more often," Laiken added, climbing on top of Rance to straddle him, preparing for another round. He chuckled again, hiding his guilty thoughts.

"I really didn't have a chance to eat at all, trying to get those cases together for the coming week," he lied.

Earlier that evening, against all he knew was right, he'd asked Feenie to meet him after hours under the guise of needing to discuss her case. Without hesitation, she agreed, asking him just to let her know where. His loins leapt when she walked into Rocco's, an Italian restaurant, dressed in a fuchsia-colored knit dress that clung to her curves. Although Feenie was a short woman, its extra-high hemline coupled with a pair of four-inch heels gave the illusion of legs that went on for days. Her hair hung around her shoulders in soft tendrils, perfectly framing her face that, regardless of her indiscretion, portrayed a sense of innocence and naivete.

"Good evening," he greeted, standing to shake her hand as she approached the table.

"Hi, Mr. Alexander."

"Just call me Rance."

"Okay," Feenie agreed as he helped her with her seat, secretly inhaling the aura of her presence.

"Have you had dinner yet? I know I proposed an awkward time to meet, just before dinner but long after lunch," he expressed nervously. "There were just a few other details that I needed to revisit with you—and please forgive me if some of these things I've asked before, but with your husband also having an attorney, it's best we prepare thoroughly, because some of the questions that could be asked could turn what I anticipate to be a fairly easy case into a nasty and painful proceeding." In all actuality, Feenie and Marvin's divorce was pretty run-of-the-mill. There were no children or assets involved other than a Hyundai Sonata with high miles that Feenie insisted on having. And because she was currently in possession of the vehicle and using it to get back and forth to work each day, it would hardly take any effort to have it awarded to her although it was in both her and Marvin's names.

"I figured I would need some professional help," Feenie responded, wiggling in her seat in search of comfort. As she crossed her legs beneath the table, her foot brushed against Rance's calf, sending a jolt of electricity straight up his leg. "Excuse me."

"You're fine." He reached beneath the table to

make a quick adjustment to his pants as he cleared his throat. "So, uh . . . you never answered my question," he probed as he repositioned himself. "Had you had a chance to grab dinner?"

"No. Actually this is perfect. Thanks for asking me to meet you."

"My pleasure. Why don't we take a minute to look over the menu before we get started?"

Easily an hour and a half slipped by the two of them, as they did more talking for pleasure than for business between mouthfuls of sautéed jumbo shrimp and scampi savoiarda. By the time the night ended, Rance's head was filled with explicit visions that he chose not to ward off.

CHAPTER 6

Present day

Nadia swore to herself it would be her last time doing this, but she just couldn't help it. She did take Pazzo out first, but shortened their normal route. As a matter of fact, as soon as he did his business, Nadia took him back to the house to begin her scavenger hunt.

"Go 'head." She ordered Pazzo to his corner once she removed his leash, then went upstairs to the bathroom to explore the medicine cabinet. Before opening it, she thought about a commercial she'd seen where a girl was in someone's bathroom being nosy just like she was about to be, glanced around nervously, then slid back the glass of the medicine cabinet. To her dismay, it was filled with marbles that spilled out all over the place. Nadia didn't let that deter her. After all, if it was filled with marbles, she would have time to pick them all up and put them back before Jonathan got back home again.

Behind the glass was general medicine cabinet stuff. A bottle of NyQuil, an open box of Alka-Seltzer cold tablets, some shaving gel, aftershave, a pack of razors, a tube of Colgate, and a large bottle of Listerine. There was one thing in particular that caught Nadia's eye, however; it was a purple zipper case with the name of some drug embroidered in white letters. She studied the words, Zyprexa-Olanzapine, taking note of the spelling so she could research what it was for once she got home. Inside the case were just some travel-sized basic toiletries, and two pens with the name of the drug printed on them. Nadia slid one of the pens from the case and put it in her pocket to use it later for research. After returning the case back to the cabinet, she wandered into Jonathan's room toward his nightstand, which was a pair of drawers and a cabinet section beneath. She slid the first drawer open and found a few ink pens with the name of his company imprinted on them, a few notepads with numbers scribbled on them, an outdated copy of *Our Daily Bread*, and a pair of earbuds, neatly wrapped and held by its own cording. The second drawer held a brown leather journal that was just begging to be picked up and peeked in, so not wanting to disappoint, that is exactly what Nadia did, randomly opening to a page.

Since my daddy left me, what else could I do but cling to my mom? Looking back over my life, I know my mom has always been there for me. Always. I still remember the look on her face when I went away to college. While she was proud of my accomplishment of getting accepted into school, the look on her face the day I hugged her and headed for my terminal has always stuck with me. It was a look of love, mixed with pride, mixed with hurt and pain that I was going so far for so long. She stood there with her bottom lip trembling, as if she would never see me again. She knew that I needed to move on in order to create a better life for myself . . . for us, and I knew that she'd want me to come back to Missouri once my educational mission was done. I've always honored her, and made sure that I called regularly while I was away. And I did miss her—bad. If I had a problem, like a little girl, I went running to my mama. When I needed advice, I'd talk to my frat brothers, but their word never soothed me like my mom's always seemed to. When I got my first job out of college, I called my mom. Just to hear her shriek with delight the way she did did wonders for my spirit. It made me feel so accomplished, so successful. I don't think I can explain it, but it meant . . . she means the world to me.

My boys thought I went too far when I stopped seeing Monica because my mom didn't like her much. She said she couldn't put her finger on it but it was just something about her. I really liked Monica too and things had been great between us. Yet I couldn't ignore my mom's intuition. Unintentionally, I started to sabotage our relationship, picking fights, being moody, indifferent, and unresponsive. When she probed for what was wrong with me, I just couldn't form the words "my mother doesn't like you." It didn't make sense that she didn't like Monica, but it did make all the difference to me, so it wasn't long before I stopped seeing her. After that, I figured the best way to handle my love life was to let my mom meet my potential love interests first. Before my emotions got involved. That's what I've been doing for ten years now. No one has passed her eyeball test. She'll talk nicely and be cordial, but the whole time, she'll be sizing a sista up. Normally, her sizing up would consist of dinner at her home. She would keep some kind of tally sheet—noting if the woman offered to help do anything, the way she sat, the way she dressed, if she addressed her as ma'am, Ms. Strickland, or Miss Lola, if her shoes made her look like a streetwalker. Then there were things that were more substantial like, if she had a child already, which honestly I tried to stay away from those, but have dated a couple that mom instantly rejected, no questions asked. If the woman didn't complete college, like she wouldn't receive a favorable mark, as she feels I need to marry someone on my level. The four things she's pointed out to me that my potential significant other should have from the gate are a job, homemaking skills, good health, and not a shopaholic who will spend up all my money, then ask for more. Funny—that is just what my mom tries to do. Nonetheless, I trust my mom to see the things that I can't see, since I am easily blinded by my interests. I'm sure she's saved me from making some bad choices in my life.

I really am trying to find a balance, though, between my mom and the women I choose to date and the decisions I make around that. I'll never forget the time I was dating Audrey, whom I hadn't taken her to meet my mom yet, but we had plans to go up to the Poconos one weekend. Well, Mom called and asked me to come home for a cookout she was throwing. I couldn't disappoint her, but I wasn't

*ready for her to tell me Audrey wasn't the one, so I
lied to Audrey and told her I had to go out of town
unexpectedly on business. When Audrey found out
I'd lied my way out of a weekend with her to eat hot
dogs and hamburgers with my mom, things ended
pretty quickly, after she called me a mama's boy.*

*And I am, but is that so wrong? She gave me life
and a whole lot more. When I compare her impor-
tance to a woman who maybe I just met or am getting to know, really there is no comparison. Who
knows if there is a true love for me? I've broken up
with so many women for so many reasons that I'll
never be able to predict whether a relationship will
work out or not, but one thing I do know for sure,
Lola loves her baby boy, and I love her right back.
That's not going to change. I think when the O'Jays
wrote that song, they had me in mind, because I will
always love my mama, and she will always be my favorite girl.*

"Whoa! Mama's boy is right." Nadia spoke to
herself. Thinking back to the muffin pan she'd
seen the other day, she could now picture
Jonathan standing in the kitchen pouring flour
and sugar in a mixing bowl while his mom
greased a couple of cake pans. *Well, let me not be
so quick to judge. After all, I've always heard that the
way a man treats his mama is the way he will treat his
wife. Hmmm. I'll have to look into that a little more.*
She thumbed through some other entries, which
were mostly brief lines that summarized his
day, and what looked like some goal planning.
Nadia put the journal back in its place, then
peeked into the cabinet section. There she found

a large Ziploc bag filled with the owner's manuals for his televisions, stereos, DVD players, and the like. There was a long phone cord neatly bundled, a flashlight, a dusty box of Stetson cologne, last year's calendar courtesy of a St. Louis barbershop, a collection of matchbooks from restaurants all around the world, and a stack of cards and letters. Making herself comfortable on the floor, she picked up the stack and began to thumb through. On top was a card whose front read "For a Special Son." Nadia skipped past that one and sorted through the other envelopes. Most were product warranty cards, company Christmas cards, and random business letters, but there was one small stationery envelope with Jonathan's name on it that also caught her eye—so of course she opened it.

Jonathan,

Hey! Hope you are enjoying the dinners especially prepared for you. Let me know which one is your favorite. I am a straightforward kind of woman, and don't believe in playing games like some of these little girls on the block, so let me just let you know the deal. I be watching how you be checking me out, and I'ma just tell you like this. Just say the word. Whatever you want you can get; no strings—I ain't got time for that. So maybe the next dinner can include a little dessert . . . I got a little hot chocolate and whipped cream.

Feenie

Nadia folded the letter, slid it back in its envelope, and bit into her lower lip. Well, one thing for sure, with Feenie having two kids, he wouldn't be taking her home to meet his mother. But still, the note was dated back to the second week he'd moved in—anything could have transpired since then. She was prompted to look into the drawer that housed Jonathan's underwear a second time, to look for condoms, particularly an open box. And in the back of the drawer, there was a gold box of Magnums, size large, which immediately impressed her. There were two missing from the unit count of twelve. Now, Nadia had never seen Feenie go over and stay any great length of time at Jonathan's house, but she knew she couldn't catch everything. But then again, suppose Jonathan was a minute man. *That would be a sad story . . . a man who needs size large who couldn't last longer than a minute or two?* The thought made Nadia literally shake her head.

Nadia left after that, both disgusted with what she considered Feenie's *trampishness,* and disappointed that maybe Jonathan was doing the do with Feenie, and that he might be putting it all down in a matter of a minute. Those thoughts impacted the way Nadia felt about ultimately accepting Jonathan's dinner invite. As interested as she had been in Jonathan, he now had a bit of tarnish on him.

Back at her place and taking a seat at her computer, Nadia stared out the window blankly, waiting for her system to boot up. Once it did, she did a Google search of Zyprexa, and gasped at the results. It was an FDA-approved medicine for treating schizophrenia or bipolar disorder. Nadia wasted no time getting Terryn on the phone.

"Okay . . . so Jonathan is crazy."

"What are you talking about this time?" Terryn said, already beginning to laugh. "If you ask me, you're the crazy one."

"No—for real, listen! He's some crazy bipolar, highly paid dog lover who is screwing Feenie!" Nowhere on Nadia's list of *Qualities of Mr. Right* did any of those things appear. "Why does it always seem like the fine ones are women beaters, pedophiles, broke, unemployed, gay, in jail, on drugs, married, stupid, got bad credit, don't have a car, live with their mamas, alcoholics, don't believe in God, or just plain crazy! I need somebody opposite all of those things."

"Girl, you had a whole list ready, didn't you? You sound like you have dated every man in the whole wide world to come up with that assessment."

"I'm serious! I'm about to start believing that there is no such thing as a good man," Nadia whined. "Because if there were, one of us would have found at least one by now."

"Chile, please, I ain't particularly looking. If something come my way that kinda got it together, that's good enough for what I'm looking for for right now."

"Well, I'm looking for somebody just like my daddy, who never hit my mama, didn't prey on kids, got money in the bank, been on his job for forty years straight, never been incarcerated, lived drug, smoke, and alcohol free, went to church every single Sunday, had perfect credit—and gets on my case about mine every chance he get—is highly intelligent, and completely single. Is that too much to ask?" Nadia wailed.

"All I'm saying is good luck with that one. Let me get off this phone, I need to prepare some documents before I get to work tomorrow. I'll talk to you later."

Although Nadia's dad had been married to her mom, Zibby, they divorced when she was ten and he never remarried. To the best of Nadia's memory Zibby ran off to Las Vegas to be with some guy named Bo with her in tow. Nadia stayed with her mom until she was twelve, and considered it to be the most miserable two years of her life. Zibby loved her daughter, but she was so busy chasing a showgirl dream and trying to get Bo to marry her, Nadia felt she hardly had time for a little girl spoiled by her daddy.

To Nadia, things were different in Vegas. Nadia wasn't used to not getting whatever she asked for, from doll babies, to clothes, to video games, to shoes, to whatever toys and games she saw advertised on Saturday mornings between cartoon shows. And the fact that she had to leave most of her things at Aidan's house, where she would visit for the summer and holidays, didn't help things. For Nadia, leaving most of her belongings was just like leaving all of it. Then to make things even more uncomfortable, Nadia had to share a bedroom with Zibby, which she didn't really mind, but when Bo came over, Nadia had to sleep on the couch. She thought it was fun initially, but after the third or fourth weekend, she longed for her own room. When Zibby moved into Bo's house, Nadia finally did have her own room, but it was so tiny, she felt as if she were living in a jail cell. Nadia remembered having a raggedy little day bed, with cardboard drawers underneath for her clothes . . . the few garments she did have. A shelf mounted on the wall right beneath a mirror served as a dresser and desk, and there was no closet. It sucked.

Every chance Nadia got, she'd asked Aidan if she could come live with him instead. And each time, he would say, "Put Mommy on the phone, baby."

"Mommy, Daddy wants you."

"What, Aidan?" Zibby would start. Instantly her hand would fly to her hip. "Nadia, get out of here." Nadia would tiptoe to her little closet of a room and listen, which wasn't hard to do. "Because she spoiled . . . you did that, not me . . . she has everything she needs, Aidan. Everything! . . . You know what, I'm getting sick of this."

While Nadia eavesdropped, she would pray to the Lord God Almighty that Zibby would hang up the phone and say, "Nadia, pack your things, you're going to live with your daddy." It took two whole years, but one day, Zibby slammed the phone down after arguing with Aidan, burst into Nadia's room, and said the words that set her free! That very next weekend, Aidan flew in to McCarran International Airport, spent three days taking his daughter around seeing sites like the Grand Canyon, Hoover Dam, and the Valley of Fire Park, then whisked Nadia away back to the comforts of her old room, friends, and the quality of life back in South Carolina until she decided to go to college in Maryland and ended up staying there.

Nadia pulled up e-mail and reread Jonathan's

dinner offer several times over as if the words were going to magically change. Rattling her fingers against the keyboard, she tried to think of what she could say to politely decline his date, although she wished she didn't have to. She didn't want to believe that Jonathan was sleeping with Feenie. And she didn't want to believe that he was half crazy half the time either. As many jogs as they'd taken together, she'd never seen him show any signs of mania or depression like the Web site decribed. But maybe his medication was keeping it all under control, she reasoned. And if he stayed on his meds, which Nadia was sure he was responsible enough to do, then he would be okay for a couple of hours—just long enough for dinner. Plus, she'd never actually seen him pop any pills. But then again, Nadia had to admit that she'd never seen him do much of anything other than go to work, come back home, and run up and down the street with his dog.

Suppose he really is gettin' it on with Feenie? Man, I wish I would have opened that door butterball naked the day she came knocking! From all this dog walking and running I've been doing, everything that was a little loose tightened up to just right, and simply because of my age, my body is way better than hers. By the time she would have picked her eyeballs up off the ground in envy, I could have been slamming the door in her face. But on second thought, maybe it was a good idea that I didn't, seeing as how he just might be poking her, and he on some kind of crazy pill drugs . . . and he's a minute man . . . maybe. "Shucks!" she said out loud as she prepared to respond to Jonathan's e-mail.

From: Aidans1babygirl@yahoo.com
To: Jonathan.Strickland@Infiniteglobalindustries.com
Subject: Dinner
Hi, Jonathan,
I am being asked to work double shifts for a number of
weeks right when you get back, so I don't think I'll be able
to squeeze in dinner.
I appreciate the invite, though, and a simple thank-you is
enough for watching Pazzo.
Nadia

Nadia wasn't sure what time it was in Dubai, but
obviously, Jonathan was up. It was only a few minutes later when his response appeared in her in-box.

From: Jonathan.Strickland@Infiniteglobalindustries.com
To: Aidans1babygirl@yahoo.com
Subject: RE: Dinner
Hi, Nadia,
I must admit that I was really looking forward to dinner
with you once I got home. I am disappointed that you
won't be able to accept my token of appreciation. Maybe
something will change in the next two weeks and you'll be
able to accommodate me.
By the way, I found a beautiful bangle here that made me
think of you. I hope you won't think me too forward for
bringing it back as a gift. After all, that is a lot of dog you
got there.
Jonathan

A bangle? Nadia thought. *Jonathan bought me a
piece of jewelry? Doesn't that mean he likes me or something? Oh, wait—he just wants to thank me for dealing
with his dog. I'll tell him no. But then suppose he gives
it to Feenie to thank her for all the dinners she's cooked.
Even worse, suppose he got both of us something—the*

exact same thing? And then gets back and forgets to take his medicine and forgets that he already gave me one, then gives me hers too, or vice versa? This is way too complicated. Nadia decided to decline the bangle too.

From: Aidans1babygirl@yahoo.com
To: Jonathan.Strickland@Infiniteglobalindustries.com
Subject: RE: RE: Dinner
Jonathan,
It's sweet of you to think of me, but that's really not necessary. Really, a simple thank-you is more than enough. Have a safe flight back.
Nadia

After she sent her response, Nadia did a quick search on Dubai jewelry and could have kicked herself. The pieces she found were unique and quite exquisite. And it wasn't like he didn't have a reason to say thank you. She started trying to think of a way that she could recall her last response. After figuring that there was no way she could tactfully ask for the bracelet back, Nadia dropped it and called her dad.

"Hey, sweet pea," Aidan answered right away.

"Hey, Daddy. I have a question."

"How much is it, Nadia?"

"What do you mean by that? I don't only call you when I need something, do I?"

"Typically that's the reason, but I have a few minutes to kill if you feel like making some idle conversation before you go for the jugular."

"Actually I had a man question."

"What is it, baby?"

"What does it mean when a man gives you jewelry?"

"What kind of jewelry? A ring?"

"No, a bracelet."

"What did he give it to you for?" he probed.

"To say thank you for babysitting his dog."

"He can't say that with his mouth?"

"Yeah, but he said he had a bracelet for me. Actually he was going to take me to dinner for the whole dog thing. The bracelet was extra . . . after I said no to dinner."

"That's right, baby girl; make 'em work. A man works for everything else he wants—his car, his house, his wardrobe. I told you that, didn't I?"

"A thousand times, Daddy."

"I'm just tryna make sure you don't forget that. Anyway, he's got some interest in you. If he just wanted to say thank you, he would have paid you. You just don't buy a woman jewelry for nothing," he commented. "Who is it?"

"The guy across the street."

"Does he have a job?"

"Of course, Daddy."

"What does he do?"

"He's some operations director or something like that."

"Well, if he's interested in you, he'd better be making a pretty penny."

"He has a six-figure salary. I know that for a fact," Nadia bragged before she thought about it.

"How do you know? He showed you his paycheck?" Aidan asked disbelievingly.

Uh-oh. Nadia knew it would have seemed odd for Jonathan to have shown her his paycheck, and since he *hadn't* shown it to her, she had to quickly think of a way that just by total happenstance she knew about his earnings, without telling her daddy that she'd been poking her nose in all kinds of places it didn't belong.

"You remember my college roommate Terryn? She did some temp work at his job in the payroll department, and she spilled the beans." The words formed and fell from Nadia's mouth as quickly as she'd thought them up.

"Something's wrong with a person entrusted to do payroll work who can't keep her mouth shut. If she'll tell you his business, what is she telling folks about yours?"

Nadia sighed inaudibly. "You're right, Daddy. Guess I didn't think about that, but you're right. I will be careful with what I share with her."

"Just be careful anyway. Not just with her."

"I will. Thanks."

"Anytime. You're doing all right otherwise?"

That was Nadia's cue to ask for a few dollars, but she passed this time. After she ended the call, she thought about what Aidan had said. Jonathan liked her!

Before she could talk herself out of it, Nadia composed one more e-mail.

From: Aidans1babygirl@yahoo.com
To: Jonathan.Strickland@Infiniteglobalindustries.com
Subject: RE:RE: Dinner
Jonathan,
On second thought . . . I will take you up on that dinner.
Nadia

Maybe that would be enough to get that brace-let back too.

CHAPTER 7

After being on foreign soil for what seemed like forever, Jonathan let out a relieved sigh as his plane touched down at BWI Airport. It had been a long but successful trip and he wanted nothing more to get home, shower in his own tub, and lie down in his own bed. On his way through the concourse, he found himself thinking about Nadia and the dinner he'd promised her. It was just a little after nine in the morning, and if he went straight home, he'd have time for a lengthy nap before their date that evening.

Jonathan stood herded around the baggage carousel checking his voice mail messages when he felt a tap on his shoulder.

"Hey, stranger, welcome home," Nadia greeted with a slight smile.

"Hey, you!" He smiled back sincerely. "What are you doing here?" Jonathan's eyes absorbed a vision of his neighbor he'd not seen before. She wore her hair in what Jonathan thought to be a wild and frizzy straw set, which was stuffed into the hood of an oversized pink Victoria's Secret sweatshirt, a pair of loose sweats, and a pair of white Nikes. She'd been watching Jonathan from afar, and before approaching him, had already pushed her large sunglasses in the pocket of her hoodie.

"I thought you might need a ride." Actually Nadia had come to see if there was anyone else there who would be meeting Jonathan off his plane. Convinced that there wasn't, she figured she'd make her drive out to the airport worth the gas money spent.

"I was actually going to grab a taxi. I thought you'd be at work today."

"Gotta get my hair done," she said, pointing to her head. "Got a hot date tonight."

"Hot, huh?" he asked. Nadia only smirked. Jonathan heaved a large black suitcase from the carousel, stood it on its wheels, and tilted it toward him. "I'm ready when you are. Did you pick a place for dinner?"

"Um . . ." She new exactly where she wanted to go, but she stalled a bit. "I think so."

"Great. What did you pick?"

"Ixia." Nadia glanced to try to capture Jonathan's reaction, but he didn't flinch.

"Did you make reservations?"

She nodded casually.

"For what time?" He hoisted his luggage into the trunk of Nadia's Mustang, then opened her car door.

"Eight."

"Cool. That gives me a little time to rest." Taking his seat on the passenger side, he dropped his head backward onto the headrest and closed his eyes. "How's Pazzo?"

"He's great."

"He give you any trouble?"

Nadia shook her head, hoping he wouldn't notice the scrubbed carpet spot in his bedroom.

"Thanks again for seeing after him."

"No problem at all."

Jonathan drifted off into a light doze while Nadia thought over Feenie's letter. If she hadn't found it, she would have picked a restaurant a little more reasonably priced than Ixia, but she wanted to see where his motives were and felt she could gauge that by how he'd spend his money . . . particularly on her.

Within the hour Nadia dropped Jonathan off and sped away to Luna's for her hair appointment. A touch-up to her roots and a wrap would give her the elegant look she was after for the evening. As she pulled into the lot, the sight of Feenie's truck both surprised and disgusted her.

"What is she doing here?" Nadia mumbled, thinking Feenie would be a better client for Bonika's kitchen getting a box perm from a drugstore shelf. "Overaged ghetto queen." She parked several spaces down, pushed her door open, and walked inside.

Sitting in the waiting area, Feenie saw Nadia come in and crinkled her nose as she ducked behind a magazine. "Nasty hoochie heifer," Feenie uttered, then returned the magazine to the table and looked at Nadia dead-on with a phony smile pasted on her face. "Hey, girl." She waved. "I ain't know you came here."

"Oh. Hi," Nadia said, barely giving any eye contact.

"What you getting done?" Feenie probed, looking at the bush of hair that framed Nadia's face.

"Just my hair."

"Yeah, girl. You need to take care uh dat!" Feenie reached to pick at a tendril of Nadia's hair, but Nadia drew back in quick defense, which offended Feenie. "Hmph! Don't nobody wanna cut their fingers on that barbwire."

"Excuse me?" Nadia gawked.

"I'm just saying you need to do something with that bird's nest."

"Jonathan likes it," Nadia chortled in response, rolling her eyes. She could have burst out in full-blown laughter from the shocked expression Feenie now wore. Her mouth hung open as if she were a baby bird at feeding time, and her eyes were stretched as wide as Frisbees. "Flies are going to get in there," Nadia added, walking off to the receptionist's desk and confirming her appointment.

"I know you aint screwin' Jonathan, 'cause he all about this right here," Feenie blurted, pointing to her crotch as soon as Nadia took a seat in the waiting area.

"Is that so?" Nadia asked, keeping her cool, but thinking back to Feenie's card and the two absent condoms.

"And just so you know, I still took him that plate," she commented. "And not only did he eat the dinner, he ate a whole lotta dessert."

Knowing now that Feenie was lying, Nadia couldn't help but laugh, starting with a little sniggle, but then bursting into a hearty chuckle.

"I don't know what you laughing for. 'Cause to

be honest with you, you's the fool. I got what I wanted out the deal—a weekend in that big ol' hotel bed he got."

Nadia slowed her chuckle, giving what Feenie had said some thought. *How would she know what kind of bed Jonathan has?*

"Yeah, we did a little something on that nice white comforter and fluffy pillows."

Nadia didn't comment or show any type of reaction. "You a nosy somebody, did you know that?" she said, discerning that Feenie was simply digging for information.

"What?" she snapped in offense.

"You heard me right." Nadia plucked a magazine from the stack and began to thumb through it.

"You the one brought Jonathan up," Feenie shrieked. "But somehow, I'm the one being nosy. Girl, please. Your business *ain't* that important." Feenie picked up the magazine she'd had earlier, but found she was unable to focus on reading at all for trying to think of something snappy to say. "And for the record, I know that Jonathan ain't thinkin' 'bout you; I don't care how much you prance around in his robe." Nadia cut her eyes over at Feenie but didn't comment. "And I'ma tell you this—"

"Feenie, I'm ready for you," her wax technician called.

"Chicken head," Feenie mumbled, lifting her purse and rising to her feet.

Feenie didn't see Nadia anymore during her visit, but was curious of truly what her involvement with Jonathan might have been. And that was what she was going to find out.

"Thank you, Feenie." Jonathan said, setting yet another plastic plate full of what he considered to be crap that he wouldn't even feed to his dog on the dining room table. "And thank you for coming by."

"You welcome." He cringed at her poor use of the English language. *It's actually you're welcome, as in you are?* Rubbing a hand over his head and pretending to yawn, Jonathan continued. "I've got a pretty long day tomorrow." It did no good; Feenie acted like she couldn't take a hint.

"Oooh, this your family?" With no fear of Pazzo, she walked over to the mantel and picked up his photos.

"Yeah," Jonathan responded, limiting his words, not wanting to contribute to her extended stay. "Look, Feenie, I—"

"Who is this right here?" Her hand flew toward a five-by-seven photo of a woman.

"My sister Adonna." He sighed inaudibly.

"She pretty."

"Thanks." Jonathan's lips were pressed tightly together, holding in a couple of choice words locked in his head instead of letting them tumble from his mouth.

"You see your family a lot?" Before he could answer, his phone started to ring.

"I'm sorry, I need to get that, but I'll see you out first."

"Oh, it's all right, I can wait. Go 'head." Feenie

shooed him with her hand, then turned back around to finish looking at pictures. This time he sighed out loud, nonetheless went to answer the phone instead of forcing her out the door. Glancing at the caller ID, Jonathan saw that it was his mother.

"Hello."

"How's my baby doing?"

"Your baby's just fine," he answered, using a tone he normally didn't take with his mother, but reserved for dealing with women he dated, or was at least interested in dating. "And how's my baby?" he threw back, hoping Feenie would get the impression that he was talking to some-one other than the woman who birthed him. In his peripheral vision he did see that she whipped her head around and stared.

"Well, when you have one, let me know," Lola Strickland chuckled.

"You know you're my baby, with your fine self. What do you need me to do for you?" Jonathan cooed playfully but convincingly enough to make Feenie roll her eyes.

That bed' not be that heifer 'cross the street, she sulked.

"First of all, I need you to tell me who you think you talking to sounding all sexed over like that. Then you can tell me whether you put that money in my account today 'cause I got a few things I need to take care of round here."

Had Jonathan not been trying to give Feenie the wrong impression, he would have argued with Lola. It seemed every other day, he was wiring and transferring funds into her account.

"Whatever you need. I'll take care of you; you know that," he forced out, maintaining his tone.

"I'm so glad to hear you say that, 'cause my doctor said I need to go on a cruise or something to relax and get my blood pressure down."

"A cruise!" He nearly choked, but then coughed to cover the surprise in his voice.

"Yeah. I need a vacation, Jonathan. Your sisters round here, 'bout to worry me to death." Lola scraped a fingernail back and forth against her scalp between two thick pepper-colored cornrows. "And 'fore I go I need to get my hair redone, 'cause it's itchin'."

"Hold on a minute." Jonathan clasped his hand over the mouthpiece and whispered over to Feenie, "I'll be a while on this call. Do you mind seeing yourself out?" This time she nodded her head quickly and tiptoed to the door.

"It's okay. I need to go get the girls anyway," she answered, tugging at her baby tee. "I'll come by a little bit later to see how you like . . ." Her voice trailed off when she noticed Jonathan had turned his attention back to his phone call.

"A cruise, huh?" he continued, purposely ignoring Feenie.

"Mmm-hmm. I need to just get away for a little while."

"Get away from what, Mama? You don't do nothing but watch Lifetime and crochet blankets. What's so stressful about that?"

"Them blankets paid your way through college," Lola snapped, offended by her son's words. "My hand's still aching from all the yarn I tied in knots so you could be where you at today!"

"Yes, ma'am," Jonathan said respectfully, bowing out of what he never intended to become an argument.

"Seem like you would be a little bit grateful. Guess now that you making all that money, you done forgot about your mama."

Her light sniffling between sentences made Jonathan roll his eyes although he felt a twinge of guilt.

"I guess I can't be but so mad; the Lord Jesus healed ten lepers and only one uh them came back and said thank you, and if they did it to the Lord and Savior, then why should I expect more?"

Jonathan sighed inaudibly. "They whipped him all night long," she continued, her voice becoming shakier with every word. "Snatched out his beard and spit in his face."

"How much is the cruise, Ma?"

"Beat 'im till they couldn't recognize 'im no more."

"How much is the cruise, Ma?" he repeated, rubbing his head.

"Naw, don't worry about it. I'll be all right. I'll find me something else to do."

"Ma, stop acting like that."

"I ain't acting like nothing. It's you that's doing the acting—acting like it's gonna kill you to gimme the money for the cruise that my doctor is telling me I need. But I know you got bills and other things you need to concern yourself with, so don't worry about me."

"Mama, how much is the cruise?" Jonathan asked a final time.

Lola puffed out her answer, although she

was filled with glee. "It ain't nothing but about fifteen hundred."

"Fifteen hundred! How much Stephanie, Adonna, and Diane contributing?"

"You know them girls ain't got no money. They doing the best they can with what they got. They ain't go to school like you and they got them babies to look after." Lola paused only for a few seconds. "They had this thing where you could register for the cruise right online, so you can go up there and pay for it instead of sending me the money to pay it," she continued, going for the close.

"What cruise line is it?" Jonathan huffed.

"Carnival. You want me to give you my registration number? You gonna need that when you go up there." Lola dug through her purse to pull out the envelope that held her power bill, which she'd jotted the information down on. "You ready for it?"

"Yes, ma'am; what is it?"

Lola blurted out a string of numbers and letters that Jonathan had to ask her to repeat twice.

"You must got some lady friend over there keeping you company since you cain't hear what I'm saying," she chuckled, happy that she'd been able to get her way.

Jonathan ignored the comment. "All right, I'll take care of this sometime this evening."

"Let me know when you do. Love you, baby."

"Love you too, Ma." Jonathan ended the call with a heavy sigh, yet logged on and pulled up the information for his mother's trip. His cheeks filled with air, then deflated again when he saw the seventeen-day South America cruise Lola had booked for herself. He started to call his mom back in protest, but thought better of it, not wanting to hear her lay a guilt trip on him a second time. "This has got to stop," he whispered to himself as he punched in his card number to finalize the trip.

It wasn't that Jonathan wasn't grateful for his mother's sacrifices in raising him and his three sisters, but she just seemed to recognize no boundaries when it came to her finances and his. Not only had Jonathan made himself responsible for his mother's insurance and health care cost, but every single month she found some extracurricular activity that required more money. Last month, it was her circle of lady friends all wanting to spend the weekend at Casino Queen. "I don't hardly ever get to get out of the house," she whined. "I spent my time in the house, raising y'all and sacrificing what I wanted to do; I just want a chance to live a little bit." Jonathan sent the money.

The month before, she wanted new carpet put in her home. "I got this same raggedy carpet that was in here when you took your first steps. Do you know how much fruit punch and potato chips and muddy shoes and Play-Doh done got mashed down in this rug? You cain't even tell what color it used to be," she complained. Jonathan sent the money.

Before that it was a new bedroom set, new dishes, new tires for her Trailblazer—top of the line, of course. "You don't want your mama skiddin' all over the streets of St. Louis, do you?" she'd said.

"Mama, I'ma have to get a second job to keep

up with you," Jonathan chuckled in jest, but his thoughts were serious.

"It's just a cruise; that ain't too much to do for the woman who gave you life, is it? I don't think it is. 'Cause I'd do anything for my mama if she was still livin', God rest her soul." Lola went on for another thirty minutes talking about how children didn't honor their parents as much as they did back in her day and what a disgrace it was. "Did you see that chile that slapped his mama in the face on the Dr. Phil show? She need for someone to give *her* a whuppin'."

Jonathan had tried an allowance system, wiring a set figure into her bank account each month, which worked for a while, but once Lola got used to the constant flow of cash, it didn't take her long to overspend and need more. Not wanting to process any more information through his exhausted mind, he decided to deal with it later, and rest up for his date.

"Woo, I gotta pee," Nadia said out loud to herself as she turned onto her street. She approached her driveway just in time to see Feenie waltzing in through Jonathan's door. Quickly she bolted inside and up the stairs to keep a watch on his front door from her window, but after glancing and dancing for three full minutes, she could no longer hold back the urge to answer nature's call. By the time she returned to the window, Feenie had gone, but Nadia hadn't seen her leave. She stayed posted for the next thirty minutes, watching and wondering. They were scheduled to go to dinner in just an hour, and there was no way she could stay glued to the window and look as stunning as she wanted to for the evening in her new $325 Tory Burch cocktail dress.

Trying to satisfy her curiosity, she stooped to crossing the street and knocking on Jonathan's door, prepared to tell him she would need an extra half hour to get ready for their date. Her knocks went unanswered as Jonathan slept peacefully, his hearing blocked by a pair of headphones he usually wore while flying. Not knowing what to make of it, Nadia came close to taking a walk down to Feenie's, but talked herself out of it.

"His loss," she reasoned, then returned to her perch at her computer, unable to peel herself away from spying. She surfed the Internet idly, making changes to her MySpace profile layout and sending comments to her contacts she hadn't reached out to in a while, then watched video after video on YouTube. Finally becoming bored with that, she sauntered to her bedroom, secured her hair with a slew of bobby pins, then covered it with a satin sleep bonnet and stripped down to her bra and panties preparing for bed. Just as she nestled into the sheets, far earlier than her bedtime, Jonathan rang her doorbell in perfect time for their date.

Nadia pulled on her robe, trod to the door, and gasped once she peered into the peephole. "Shoot!" she whispered, wondering what to do. There was no way she could allow Jonathan to see her in her current state. She cursed herself for not having showered the minute she'd gotten home, but she'd been so focused on looking for Feenie, nothing could draw her away. Snatching the bonnet from her head and stuffing it into her pocket, she decided to open the door. As much as she could she put on a sullen expression, wrapped one arm around her waist, stood behind her door, and cracked it a bit.

"Oh, hi, Jonathan," she barely whispered as she read his expression of surprise mixed with confusion.

"Uh, hi. I thought we . . ." He glanced down at his wrist to make sure he wasn't too early or too late. "I thought we were going out to dinner tonight." He formed this more as a question than a statement.

"Right. I walked over to your house to tell you I wasn't really feeling well, but you didn't answer," she said, telling a half-truth. "Then I tried to call, but you weren't answering the phone either," she added.

"Did you? I'm so sorry. I must have been still asleep." Jonathan slid his hands into his pockets as a few seconds passed. "You sure look nice for a woman who's not feeling well."

"Thanks." Nadia added a small cough for effect. "Do you mind if I take a rain check on dinner?"

"No, not at all. Do you need me to get you anything, some soup or some Alka-Seltzer or something? I got a few things at the house that might make you feel better."

"Um . . . maybe some soup and juice would be nice."

Jonathan bobbed his head slowly as he backed

away. "Okay. I'll be back in a little bit, then—maybe twenty minutes? In the meantime, you go lie down and try to feel better."

"Thanks, Jonathan."

"You're welcome."

CHAPTER 8

Ten years earlier

It had only taken two more dinners before Feenie used the power of seduction to lure Rance to her bed. And like a mouse poking its nose into a spring-loaded trap, Rance got a little more than what he'd bargained for.

He immensely enjoyed Feenie's uninhibited sexuality, as she did things that his wife had stopped doing long ago. Whenever Rance came around, Feenie made him feel like a king, although her surroundings were meager at best—a small one-bedroom apartment with a double bed purchased from a hotel's going-out-of-business liquidation sale. But she kept it neat and clean, and found other ways to make Rance feel luxuriously pampered and spoiled.

She would always cook for Rance when he came by, believing that the way to a man's heart and wallet was through his belly. And after filling him up at the table, she'd allow him to fill her up in the bedroom. She insisted that Rance use a condom, although she'd long before told him that since she'd lost her first child she'd been unable to conceive. It was her way of manipulating his mind into believing that the pregnancy she was secretly planning would be a complete "mistake."

Feenie hadn't started planning a pregnancy, however, until Rance loosened his purse strings. It started with Feenie mentioning to him that she wanted to prepare a special meal for him but couldn't quite afford the ingredients.

"Well, what is it that you were thinking of cooking?" he asked, running a hand up and down her bare back as they lay entangled between the sheets.

"I wanted to try my hand at this recipe I saw on TV; rack of lamb in a mustard and Jamaican rum coating, with some green peppercorn and candied pistachio sauce, and some grilled asparagus spears and baked potatoes with pesto dipping sauce," she whispered into his ear between kisses.

"You know how to cook like that?" he asked, responding to her kisses by pressing his lips against hers.

"Everything I do, I do it well. Don't you think so?" She slid beneath the covers to prove her point, causing Rance's eyes to roll back into his head before they closed. When she slid back up his body and let him out of her den of deceitful passion, he'd left her five hundred dollars.

"Get the foods you need, and why don't you pick up a little something for yourself?"

That had been all Feenie needed to hear.

Over the next six months, she played her cards right, being at Rance's beck and call, showing up at his office after hours. She even role-played, pretending to be his assistant "Mi-mi," coming in for her regular shift clad in the tiniest skirt she could find, tops that barely covered her breasts, and platform heels. Several nights per week, Rance explained to his wife that he'd be working late, but invited her to call the office anytime. Initially, that was exactly what Laiken did, thinking she smelled a rat, but after calling several times and always getting her husband, she soon became secure and believing of his story. The few times that Laiken did pop by the office with a picnic basket full of dinner items, without even being asked, Feenie hid herself in an extra office, allowing Rance to manage his wife and his home life. She knew a money train when she saw one and wasn't willing to sacrifice its benefits for a confrontation with a woman Rance went home to every night.

Rance, appreciating Feenie's skilled discretion, responded by giving her more cash, sometimes per her request, but most of the time just because. He was being sexed out of his mind and wanted to keep a good thing going. But once Feenie got ready for more, she did away with the pill and let Rance release inside her, knowing she'd be set for life.

"Rance, we need to talk," she started after easing down off his desktop one evening. Rance was hot, sweaty, and exasperated from the labor he'd just put in, and had all but collapsed into his chair. He motioned with a wave of his fingers for Feenie to come close to him. She straddled his lap, and he, like a newborn baby, latched on to her breast and let out a satisfied moan.

"What is it?" he mumbled, his mouth full of her flesh.

"Rance." She paused as if she struggled to get her words together. "Rance, I'm late."

Immediately, his suckling stopped and he leaned back in his chair. "What do you mean?"

"I mean I'm late," she repeated. "My cycle hasn't started." Feenie bit into her lower lip and studied Rance's face, which was now filled with worry.

"So . . . so, what are you going to do?" he asked, knowing there was no way on the green earth he wanted her to have his baby.

Feenie shrugged, although her plan was in full effect. "You know I've always longed for a baby, and thought after Marvin did what he did to me that it would never happen." Rance kept silent. "And now I may be expecting and I just feel . . . I don't know. I just feel like this is a second chance for me."

In a low and as gentle a tone as possible, Rance replied, "Feenie, you know I can't tell Laiken that you're . . . we're having a baby." He rubbed a hand over his face, now wanting Feenie off his lap, but thought more strategically than to push her off, knowing full well that she could easily blow his cover. He tilted his head back and studied the ceiling tiles above them.

"I really want this baby, Rance. I don't expect you to leave your wife and kids, but I really want this baby." Feenie began to cry. "Please don't ask me to get rid of it, because I just can't do that."

Rance cursed himself silently.

"This baby means more than anything to me and if it means staying out of your life in order to keep it, then that is what I'm willing to do." At that, Feenie pulled away from Rance, standing to her feet. "I don't mind giving you up Rance, but I can't give up my baby," she said through tears as she slid her arms into the sleeves of the trench coat she'd arrived in, tightened its belt around her waist, and headed for the door. Before leaving she turned back to say some final words. "I'll send you the doctor's bills and what we'll need financially, but other than that, you don't have to worry about me ruining your life."

A week later, Rance received a certified letter to his office that contained a copy of Feenie's proof of pregnancy, the doctor she'd chosen, and the estimated cost to deliver the baby if there were no complications, and an exorbitant monthly dollar amount that Feenie had outlined she'd need to take care of herself and keep Rance's secret. Rance blew a puff of air from his cheeks and filed the documents away, placing them under lock and key.

Feeling like Feenie had his arm twisted behind his back, he punched figures into a calculator, budgeting in her demands. He had no choice but to pay them. Laiken was a great wife, and then there were his two boys, David and Michael, ages two and three respectively. He spent an extra hour in his office after closing, this time not being entertained, but thrashing himself with his thoughts of how he'd been so foolish. A million couldas, shouldas, wouldas went through his head. Why had he stopped using the condoms Feenie once insisted on? Why had he allowed himself to become involved with her in the first place? Why didn't he stop after the first time? They were all questions that he didn't have the answers to, and even if he did, it wouldn't change anything. He was going to have to bite the bullet and pay it forward.

As long as Rance sent a check in a timely fashion, a check every week, he wouldn't hear a peep from Feenie, other than her monthly mailing of bills and updates. But the few times he'd forgotten, she quickly let it be known by a nasty and to-the-point phone call that she held his destiny in the palm of her hand.

Rance thought several times of just coming clean with his wife and facing the consequences at home. Especially when he received the letter that there wasn't just one baby, but there were two. Along with that letter was a request for twice the amount of money Feenie had demanded before. Rance left work early that day, headed to the golf driving range, and with several aggressive strokes, accented with curse words, worked through his initial anger, knowing that he truly could be angry with no one but himself. He stayed on the range for nearly four hours, hitting ball after ball until he could barely lift his arms.

Laiken, instantly noticing the stress her husband wore on his face, tried to ease away his troubles, which he dared not share with her, but he pushed her away, stating that he needed to be alone.

Feenie, on the other hand, was almost living the life that she'd dreamed about since high school. While Rance's seventeen hundred dollars a month didn't compare to the millions she'd planned on having at her disposal had Marvin gone on to the NBA, it was acceptable. With a few months of saving, she began renting a well-kept single-family home, bought a late-model vehicle, and sat on her behind rubbing her belly, which expanded daily with the growth of her two girls.

Feenie delivered the girls without Rance's presence, and as usual sent her certified package containing photos and copies of the hospital replica of their birth certificates, reading Carance Alexander and Mirance Alexander, July 4, 2000. Along with it came a significant financial stipend increase. Rance looked at the pictures in disdain, not because of the babies—they were the most precious things he'd ever laid eyes on—but because of Feenie's gloat-filled beaming. He cringed at the sight of her face, wishing he'd never met her. Nonetheless, every week like clockwork, a deposit was made into Feenie's bank account.

Rance hadn't gotten the opportunity to meet his daughters until their second birthday. Feenie held back no expense, throwing a two-day event, since it was both a national holiday and the girls' birthday. She started on Friday night with a backyard barbecue that was more suited for adults than two two-year-old toddlers. Feenie invited everyone she knew to come over for flame-cooked steaks, shrimp and vegetable kabobs, grilled chicken and andouille, burgers with spicy mayo and caramelized onions, and hot dogs for the kids. Along with liquor, beer, and wine, she served a spectacular pineapple and rum drink, which was a mixture of peach and apricot nectar, pineapple juice, fruit punch, dark rum, and fresh lime juice, garnished with sliced strawberries and pineapple spears. For dessert, there were ginger-accented biscuits topped with warm spiced plums and whipped cream alongside a standard sheet cake and Hi-C drink boxes for the kids.

"Feenie, girl, you sure know how to throw a party!" her mom commented, sipping on her third glass of the spirited beverage of her choice. "You might ain't got a million dollars, but you right next to it! That man is taking good care of his kids."

Feenie and her guests partied well into the night after the girls were long asleep.

The next day, Feenie gave them a standard Chuck E. Cheese's party, which didn't even cost one-quarter of the shindig she'd hosted the night before. It was there that Rance first laid eyes on his daughters. Bringing his sons with him, he released them to play, then waltzed over to the party area and watched from afar, easily identifying the set of beautiful twins, with wavy black hair hanging in ringlets, pink shorts, and white T-shirts with "I'm a Princess" printed across the front. He and Feenie caught eyes but didn't speak a word. He eased over and took a seat at a neighboring table, awaiting his pizza order, but couldn't peel his eyes away from the two mulatto children he'd fathered.

Taking the girls to the bathroom, Feenie stopped at his table.

"Hey." She spoke with no feeling.

"How are you?"

"Great."

Rance's eyes bounced back and forth between his daughters as they hugged their mother, one wrapped around each leg. "Those are some gorgeous girls you have there," he commented, longing to pick them up.

"Thanks. I had a little help."

"Is there anything you need?" he said, moved purely by his emotions.

"I'll let you know. Come on, Cara and Mia," she said, lifting the twins into her arms. He didn't see the twins again for another year, and then another year after that, although they constantly stayed on his heart and mind. Still, he knew he needed to maintain the stable home life he'd already built with his first family, so he kept the money flowing into Feenie's pocket.

It wasn't until the girls turned six that he actually had true interaction with them. Telling Laiken and the boys he needed to be away on business, he headed to Paramount's King's Dominion, an amusement park, for the weekend. As promised, Feenie met him there, girls in tow, excited about the day ahead of them. The introduction and acceptance of Rance went surprisingly well to both the parents, and within an hour, they were calling him daddy and dragging him off to various rides. By the time the sun went down and fireworks went up, the bond had been sealed. Since then, he frequently made calls to Feenie's house to talk with them, and Feenie set no boundaries for them accepting his calls, other than that they were not to speak to him when she wasn't home.

Present day

Feenie dialed Rance's office, wondering why he'd been calling her home so frequently lately.

"Alexander Law Group," Terryn answered on the third ring.

"Mr. Alexander please."

"May I tell him who's calling?"

"Ms. Trotter." Seconds later Rance was on the line.

"Feenie, help me understand why Mia and Cara are being left alone at home every weekend," he nearly yelled.

"Excuse me?" Feenie denied in her tone.

"You heard me right. Why are my girls being left unattended?" he asked a second time.

"I don't know what you're talking about," she replied coolly.

"Yes, you do and I will tell you this much, Jerrafine Trotter. If something happens to my daughters, I will make sure that you are thrown *under* the jail!" Rance slammed the handset into the cradle on his desk, unaware that Terryn had been listening right outside his door.

Daughters? she questioned in her mind. *Rance has sons, when did he get daughters?* She tiptoed to her desk and jotted on a sticky note the names she heard Rance call out: Jerrafine Trotter, Mia, and Cara.

"Mr. Alexander, I'm leaving for the evening," she announced.

"Have a good night," he responded from his office.

Terryn left, her mind in a whirlwind of thoughts about her boss's secret life.

CHAPTER 9

Oh my goodness! What am I going to put on? Nadia thought in a slight panic. "I can't just sit around in my panties and bra and this raggedy Wal-Mart robe, but I can't overdress either. And I don't want any stupid soup! I really wanted lobster tails with a baked potato and something else expensive," she retorted to herself. She dove into the shower for not even a full three minutes, focusing on what she called her hot spots and bird-bathing the rest of her body. After patting dry, Nadia spritzed on the first body splash she could wrap her fingers around, then dug through her pajama drawer for a pair of light blue cotton pants adorned with white clouds and a white T-shirt that read "sweet dreams."

Next she released her hair from what seemed to be ninety-nine bobby pins that held it in a wrap formation, and brushed it all down to frame her face. Checking her appearance in the mirror, she assessed that she did look rather cute to be sick. Nadia stood for the next several seconds making faces at herself, trying to look sullen. Just as she finished doing a running sweep of her living room, picking up odds and ends and stuffing them in the nearest closet, the doorbell chimed again. In her sick voice she answered, "Who is it?" Jonathan replied, and she opened the door slowly as if she were nearing death and could barely move.

"Wow!" he said. "You look pretty remarkable to be under the weather." He held a plastic bowl with a sealed lid filled with what looked like vegetable soup, something square wrapped up in aluminum foil, and two bottles of orange juice balanced on top.

"Well, I wish I felt remarkable." In all actuality, she did feel pretty good. "Come on in."

Jonathan shut the door behind himself, then followed her into the kitchen. "Let me grab a couple of bowls," she offered.

"No, if you just point me to them, I'll take care of it. You just take a seat," he countered.

Nadia let out a sigh for effect. "Normally, I would argue, but I don't have the strength." She feigned exhaustion as she sauntered toward her living room, pointing a weak finger behind her. "Look in that cabinet right there." With her back to him, she smiled to herself, then folded in her lips to force the smile away. Jonathan joined her about five minutes later. Utilizing a serving tray Nadia kept on the countertop, he brought in two bowls of soup, a saucer with grilled cheese sandwiches cut in half, and the juice poured into two glasses. He slid the tray onto the coffee table, then took a seat beside her.

"I'm really sorry that you're feeling so poorly."

"Thanks," she mumbled. "I'm sorry that you got dressed for nothing."

"Don't worry about it." He waved dismissively. "Sometimes staying in is better than going out anyway. I eat out all the time when I'm on the road."

"I can't say that I get to enjoy that luxury," she responded. "Must be nice." Nadia filled her mouth with a spoonful of soup that tasted nothing like the lobster she really had an appetite for, but it was tasty just the same. "Thanks for doing this for me."

"My pleasure." He nodded. "Do you mind if I turn on the TV?"

"Not at all. We can watch the encore presentation of the BET awards. I've not had a chance to see it yet."

"You watch that?"

Right away Nadia detected a bit of contempt in his voice. "Who doesn't?" she shrugged. "It's black entertainment at its best, I think."

"Really," he said as a statement. "You need to get out a little more."

"What do you mean by that?" she asked, trying not to take offense. "Wait, hold on—this is my girl." Keyshia Cole took the stage, dressed in a white shorts outfit and white thigh-high stiletto boots. Before she realized it, Nadia was popping her fingers and singing along with her. Jonathan just shook his head. Once she and Lil' Kim finished their performance song, Nadia continued where she'd left off. "So, as I was saying—what do you mean by that?"

"I'm just saying there is more to black entertainment than half-dressed women in high-heeled boots who really can't sing."

"What?"

"I mean, look at those two. You can go to any strip club and see that kind of stuff going on. And what was with all that huffing and puffing Keyshia was doing? Was that actually singing?"

"Yeah!" Nadia rushed to Keyshia's defense. "She's not signed to a label for nothing."

"Well, I don't know what she signed for, but if you asked me, singing is not it." He frowned even more at Nelly's and Lil' Wayne's performances, shunning their exposed undergarments and bare chests. "This is entertainment to you?"

Nadia didn't try to defend this time. *He kinda has a point*, she reasoned in her mind.

"Do you want to watch something else?" she asked. It was clear that she wasn't going to enjoy the show with him there. "I can watch this another time, I guess."

"That's up to you." He took a swallow of juice as he looked pensively at Nadia. "Let me ask you something. Would you actually consider dating a brother who didn't have the frame of mind to wear his pants up around his waist?" Nadia's eyes darted around the ceiling as she gave it some thought. Noting her hesitancy, he answered for her. "You would," he concluded, bobbing his head.

"You didn't even give me a chance to answer," Nadia retorted, sitting up from her reclined position.

"Just the fact that you are thinking about it says a lot." Jonathan shook his head as he pressed his lips together. "You know, I never would have pegged you as the kind of woman who is attracted to a thug." He let out a chuckle that spoke more of his disappointment than his amusement. "You women are funny."

"Funny like what?"

"Funny like you will take a man with sagging pants, gold teeth, and a nappy head calling you all out of your name before you'd look twice at a brother making an honest living in a suit and tie who chooses to treat you with integrity and respect."

"Don't you think you're being a little judgmental?" She winced. "Just because I wanted to think about my answer first doesn't mean anything." Nadia's brow furrowed in offense.

"Why would you even need to think about it? What attracts a woman to a man who takes pleasure in calling her a bitch and doesn't have the decency or self-respect to take pride in his appearance? There he is, singing about licking on a quote-unquote lollipop, and women respond by buying his albums and twisting and shaking as if the song personifies them perfectly. And then on top of that, consider the stereotype that it sets for the black man in general. It's difficult enough for us to be taken seriously in corporate America—trust me, I know. Then to have to prove my intelligence nearly every day, because of the image of black men so widely portrayed everywhere you look." Jonathan sighed. "I just never thought that you were the type of woman that found that style of man attractive."

"I never would have thought of you as the type of man who enjoys spending his free time having dinner with an ol'-school skank like Feenie," Nadia shot back, but her words didn't have the impact she thought they would, as Jonathan burst into laughter. He set his soup bowl on the table and fell back in the couch.

"What's so funny about that?" Nadia narrowed her eyes, ready to debate although confused by his laughter.

"You sure do know a lot about what goes on at my house," he said between chuckles.

"I guess I do, seeing as how I had to babysit your dog for a month and a half!" Nadia felt her blood beginning to boil as her neck began swiveling her head in sista-girl circles, showing off the body of her freshly done hair.

"And I offered to thank you I don't know how many times, but you refused. All the way down to pretending that you were sick tonight." He ended his laughter and raised his brows, beckoning a response.

"I . . . I . . ." No words would come to Nadia's mind after that single word regardless of the fact that mentally she was in a furious search for something to say.

"You know what? Don't even worry about it. You didn't want to go; you told me that from the beginning, and I should have listened. And I guess I now know why—maybe if I had the waist of my pants circling my legs we could talk." He slapped his hands against his thighs and rose to his feet. "Go ahead and enjoy the soup. I'll let myself out."

Nadia wanted to stop him, but was too stunned to move. This wasn't how the evening was supposed to go. He was supposed to stay and work out a new day for her to redeem her dinner rain check. Or at least offer to rub her feet or something! *Did I just hand this man over to Feenie?* she thought after hearing her front door close. *Oh, but wait . . . he's on the bipolar meds. Maybe they were just beginning to wear off or something. That has to be what it is.* Almost knocking over her soup as she jumped up from the couch, Nadia jetted to her living room window and peeked through the curtains. She was relieved to see him walking into his own front door, eased away, then picked up the phone to call Terryn.

"You will never believe what happened," Nadia started as soon as Terryn answered.

"And you won't believe what I found out about my boss, but you go first."

Nadia let the events of her evening tumble from her lips. "Then he just left," she exclaimed.

"So, let me get this straight. Instead of getting dressed and going out to dinner with the man, you decided to play sick and eat soup."

"Yeah, 'cause I thought he was cooped up in the house with old-tail Feenie!"

"What is her real name again?"

"Girl, I don't know. All I know I mighta just handed Jonathan over to her all because Lil' Wayne and them can't pull their pants up!" Terryn started laughing. "It's not funny, Terryn."

"Yes, it is. All you had to do is open the door and tell him you needed fifteen more minutes. He lives right across the street; he would have waited."

"Maybe he would have, but I didn't think to do that, and now he's mad at me."

"He'll be all right."

"What do you think about what he said about men in suits versus men in baggy pants?" Nadia sought.

"You know a man in a suit just does something to me anyway, but I think he made some good points. How often do you see a black professional male portrayed?" Terryn asked, but didn't wait for a response. "I mean, really, think about it. There are not that many in comparison to the rappers and stuff. And then the mess they sing about is ridiculous and degrading."

"All right, all right. I don't feel like another lecture. I still can't believe he up and left like that," Nadia sulked. "Do you think I should apologize?"

"For what?"

"For saying that he was gettin' it with Feenie."

"I don't know, maybe he needs to apologize for saying you like thugs—but look," she said as a way to segue into her own topic. "I found out today my boss has some extra children," Terryn spilled.

"Extra children? What do you mean?"

"I mean this lady called there and asked to speak to him, and I heard him ask her about his daughters, but he only has two sons by his wife."

Nadia huffed out enough air to inflate a twelve-inch balloon in one breath. "I'm having a Jonathan crisis right now. Who cares about your boss and his illegitimate kids?"

"Girl, please. If Jonathan wants you, he'll come back. And if he wants Feenie, so what? That means he was never really interested in you in the first place," Terryn summed up.

"Deg. Break me down easy, why don't you?"

Nadia said, rolling her eyes. "So, why do you care so much about your boss's philandering ways anyway? You really ought to stop being so nosy before they fire your behind."

"'Cause I think his baby mama lives down the street from you."

"So?" Nadia swallowed a mouthful of soup, frowned at its cooled temperature, then padded to her microwave to warm it up.

"I think it's Feenie."

"Get to the part why I should care. You should taste this soup Jonathan made. It is so good." Another spoonful of Italian sausage, potatoes, and kale in a creamy broth slid into Nadia's mouth. "Mmm."

"And that's exactly why you should care. If you want Jonathan so bad, this might help you out."

Suddenly Nadia took interest in what Terryn had to share. "Okay, I'm listening. What you got?"

"Now, I don't have it all together yet, but I think those two girls she has are his, because a couple of weeks ago when I was coming to your house, I swore I saw his Mercedes cruising down your block, but I didn't really think anything of it. And aren't her daughters mixed?"

"Yeah, they are, but that doesn't mean he's the daddy."

"Okay, but someone named Jerrafine called the office today, and he was asking her about why his girls were being left at home alone. Feenie got two girls, and I know I saw him driving through there. Have you ever seen those kids' daddy?"

Now that she was thinking of it, she had to admit that she hadn't . . . ever. And she'd been keeping a pretty close watch on things over the past few months. "No. Can't say that I have."

"Exactly. Because he can't make it known that he has a second family. A black one at that."

"I think it's a stretch, to be honest with you. There could be plenty of Jerrafines in the world with two little girls."

"How many Jerrafine Trotters do you know?"

Nadia turned the corners of her lips downward in thought. She had seen a few pieces of discarded junk mail at the mailboxes with that name on it.

"With two girls that live in Baltimore."

"Okay, Terryn, I still don't see how this is supposed to help me."

"Maybe it won't, but I'm just wondering what is wrong with my boss! He done ran out of here and had some babies by someone that is not his wife. I'm going to look in the files tomorrow and see if he used to represent her or something. Girl, you know I'm trying to write me a book. This is the stuff that books are made of!"

"You a nosy somebody," Nadia commented.

"Well, isn't that the pot calling the kettle black?"

"What have you two been telling your daddy?" Feenie started in on her girls as soon as she hung up the phone.

"Nothing, Mommy," Cara answered right away. Mia was silent although Feenie stared hard at her. "He called the other day, but we didn't even talk to him, because we didn't answer the phone because you weren't here," Cara lied.

"How did he know y'all were home by your-selves?" Feenie threw out, waiting for them to trap themselves into saying that they'd talked to Rance.

"I don't know. We didn't tell him that," Cara replied again.

"Somebody told him something," Feenie in-sisted, "and if y'all don't want your little tails tore up, y'all better let my business stay in this house! Do you hear me?"

"Yes, ma'am," they both answered in unison. Mia stood staring at her feet and twisting her fin-gers, while Cara looked at her mother dead-on.

"Go to bed," Feenie ordered, and immediately the two girls marched up the stairs. "And I better not hear no playing!"

"Yes, ma'am," they responded again.

Once in their bedroom, they began a whis-pered discussion.

"I told you not to call him," Mia started.

"He said we can call him any time we wanted," Cara argued.

"Yeah, but you know Mommy don't like us to talk to him when she's not home."

"So what? Mommy don't like a lot of things. I don't even think Mommy likes us."

"Yes, she does," Mia replied.

"I bet she doesn't. How much you wanna bet?"

"I don't have any money."

"Okay, if I'm right, then I will make your bed up for you all week." Cara leaned over the side of her top bunk to meet her sister's eyes.

"Okay, but how you gonna prove that she don't like us?"

"She don't because she don't never want to take us anywhere with her."

"That's because she be going to places where kids can't go," Mia expressed, pulling her comforter up to her chin.

"But she don't never take us to the places where kids can go like to the park or skating, or to Chuck E. Cheese's like Daddy does. He takes us to fun places. That is what grown-ups do when they like kids. All Mommy ever does is yell at us."

Mia didn't respond, feeling that Cara had a good argument but wanting to give her mother the benefit of the doubt. Rance made it a point to see his girls once a month, feeding all kinds of lies to his wife and boys, but feeling that it was worth it to be with his two princesses for a couple of hours.

"All Mommy wants us to do is wash the dishes," Cara said. "That is why I'ma ask Daddy if we can come live with him. I bet he'll say yeah."

"That would be so fun!" Mia gleamed, thinking of the possibilities. "We could ask him to—"

"I said go to bed!" Feenie yelled from the foot of the stairs.

The girls didn't speak another word and soon drifted off to sleep.

An hour later, Feenie tiptoed up the stairs and into her girls' room to make sure they were soundly off to sleep. Confident that they were, she slinked to her own bedroom, showered, and dressed in a sequined halter top and a super miniskirt. She slid her feet into a pair of black thigh-high boots, added a few pieces of jewelry and a little makeup, then headed out the door

for Club One. It was Ladies' Night Out on Fore-
play Thursdays, and since the drinks were half
off until midnight, she wouldn't mind paying for
one or two just in case she didn't happen to meet
anyone. She sped away to Saratoga Street, never
taking note of Rance's Mercedes parked on the
street just a couple of houses away.

He was pretty sure that the girls were once again
home alone, as they had told him about in times
past. Assuming they were asleep, he pulled onto
the road behind Feenie and trailed her until she
arrived at the club, snapping photos of her, her
truck, and its license plate. Rance was still unsure
what he planned to do with the knowledge he had,
or better yet how he could use it without blowing
his cover at home or having the girls taken away
and awarded to state custody. But if something
happened to those girls, he would never be able to
forgive himself.

After watching her get out of her vehicle, and
snapping a shot of her doing so, he drove home
beside himself with both fury and worry. Pulling
up in front of his home, he sat in the driver's seat
for more than an hour thinking about what it was
he could do. If he called Child Protective Services, surely they would remove the girls from the
house and then where would they be? If he didn't
call, who knows what would happen while Feenie
was away shaking her behind in the middle of the
night? The house could catch fire, an intruder
could break in, one of the girls could get thirsty
in the middle of the night and tumble down the
stairs. Though intimidated by his thoughts, he
wasn't moved enough to go into his house and

tell his wife of twelve years that he had a set of twins across town. That would be his career, his reputation, his family, everything he'd worked hard all his life for, gone down the drain. Laiken would take him for every dime Feenie wasn't already taking him for. Even if he tried to pass it off as a onetime affair, there would be no explaining the years of deceit and lies.

Sliding his digital camera back into its case, he stuck it under the driver's seat, pulled it out again and put it under a stack of envelopes that were nestled in the armrest's storage compartment. Rance made a mental note to upload the photos to his work computer and clear them from his camera as soon as possible. The last thing he needed was for Laiken to find the suspect snapshots.

CHAPTER 10

From: Aidans1babygirl@yahoo.com
To: Terrynsworld@gmail.com
Subject: FWD: Maybe
Hey, Terryn,
Look at this e-mail Jonathan sent me. Tell me what
you think.

From: Jonathan.Strickland@globalindustries.com
To: Aidans1babygirl@yahoo.com
Subject: Maybe
Maybe I was being a little judgmental. I'm sorry if I
offended you. I would offer to make it up to you over
dinner, but I know how you feel about that already.
Ha-ha. Maybe we can do something different.
J.

From: Terrynsworld@gmail.com
To: Aidans1babygirl@yahoo.com
Subject: RE: FWD: Maybe
You should go out with him at least once.
Your neighbor came flying into the office today raising all
kinds of sand at Mr. Alexander. She was going OFF on him.

I couldn't get the whole story, but it was something about her going to a club and something about him being a nosy #$%, pencil you-know-what so and so!

From: Aidans1babygirl@yahoo.com
To: Terrynsworld@gmail.com
Subject: RE: RE: FWD: Maybe
You better stop being a nosy #$% so-and-so before you find yourself out of a job. Who cares if they got some business together? I don't. I have my own life to live. Where should 1 let Jonathan take me? Somewhere expensive! He can afford it.

From: Terrynsworld@gmail.com
To: Aidans1babygirl@yahoo.com
Subject: RE: RE: RE: FWD: Maybe
Just say yes and let him pick the place. That way you can tell how much money he is willing to spend on you without you prompting him. How do you know he can afford it? If he got so much money, why is he living out there with y'all?

From: Aidans1babygirl@yahoo.com
To: Terrynsworld@gmail.com
Subject: RE: RE: RE: RE: FWD: Maybe
What is that supposed to mean? We broke or something? Anyway, he said he lives out here because it's a nice neighborhood and he is not ready to invest a whole lot in a home yet because he spends too much time on the road. Since you need to know so bad. I think you just mad 'cause you don't live out here with us.

From: Terrynsworld@gmail.com
To: Aidans1babygirl@yahoo.com
Subject: RE: RE: RE: RE: RE: FWD: Maybe
Whatever. If your daddy wasn't paying your rent every

other month, you wouldn't be living there yourself. You so spoiled! Girl, if my daddy would pay my bills like your daddy pays yours, I'd be staring out the window all day and night too.

From: Aidans1babygirl@yahoo.com
To: Terrynsworld@gmail.com
Subject: Whatever!!
You're such a hater.

From: Aidans1babygirl@yahoo.com
To: Jonathan.Strickland@globalindustries.com
Subject: RE: Maybe
Dinner would be nice. Friday at seven? You pick the place.
N.

From: Jonathan.Strickland@globalindustries.com
To: Aidans1babygirl@yahoo.com
Subject: RE: RE: Maybe
Looking forward to it.

CHAPTER 11

For the first time, Feenie felt intimidated by a man. Rance had called her over to his office, and not knowing what to expect, but planning to net a few hundred dollars out of the visit if possible, Feenie went dressed in a see-through black rouched blouse over a strapless bra and a tight-knit black skirt that clung to her curves and made it obvious that she had on either a thong or no panties at all. She and Rance hadn't been intimate since she'd been pregnant, but neither had they been alone together.

In her mind, she thought Rance would maybe want to talk about some upcoming secret getaway he wanted to take the girls on, or complain about the more than two grand he was shelling out each month in hush money that made it possible for Feenie to not have to work. She couldn't have been further from the truth.

"I need you to explain to me why I'm paying you all this money and you're leaving my girls home alone like they are teenagers," he started, folding his fingers together and keeping his composure. He leaned back in his leather high-backed chair and stared intently at Feenie's eyes, which were suddenly stretched wide.

"What are you talking about, Rance? Who done filled your head with some garbage about me? Everybody got something to say about what I'm doing," she threw back, unmoved by his accusation.

"You know exactly what I'm talking about." He pushed his computer monitor around to show Feenie the pictures that he'd captured sitting out in front of her home. There was a photo of the girls climbing out of Feenie's truck toting grocery bags and going into the house, then shots of Feenie leaving and ending up at the club.

"You been spying on me!" she asked incredulously, narrowing her eyes into slits.

"I've been watching how you handle my children." His tone was firm and unwavering.

"*Your* children? Excuse me? You talking 'bout the same two little girls that you are so scared are going to mess up your life?" She waved her hands frantically to emphasize her point. "The same children that you ashamed to admit to having? The same kids that can't go over to their own daddy's house 'cause he got a wife and he don't want her to know nothing about them? You got a lot of nerve calling *my* daughters *your* children," she stated louder than was comfortable to Rance.

"You need to keep it down, Jerrafine," he said sternly.

"Oh, you call me to your office and accuse me of some misfit mother crap but you want me to keep it down? I wish I would be quiet! And you wasn't asking me to tone it down when we were in this same office making those girls, were you?" she screamed even louder.

Terryn stood on the outside of the door with her hand covering her mouth.

"But I guess this is just like you to want to play the quiet game, huh? Because you know you'd be ruined if that wife of yours found out you have a second family."

"Feenie, please. This is between us; this office isn't but so big, and your voice carries. Please lower your voice," Rance asked a second time, regretting that he'd called her to his office in the first place.

"No, it's not just between us. It's between us and my two daughters, who are being given second best, while you sit up in your house on the hill giving your two sons the best of everything. That makes it between us and the girls. Your wife is driving around in a Lexus, thinking she has a faithful man, while you have me diving between bushes tryna stay outta her sight. Well, you know what, Rance Alexander? I'm getting a little sick of living like that, so guess what? If you want to call the people on me, you better be prepared to take these girls into your precious little untouchable, unblemished home!" she finished.

Hearing a bit of scuffling, Terryn backed into the hallway bathroom just in case the door opened suddenly.

"Feenie, I'm warning you. Don't leave my daughters home alone again, or the next time you talk to me, it's going to be to ask me to defend you for child neglect charges."

"If you think I'm shaken by that, then you think I'm crazy."

When Feenie opened Rance's office door, she nearly knocked Terryn over in her haste to break out of the main doors and onto the sidewalk. By the time she took a seat in her car, she'd broken out in a complete sweat, worried that Rance would call the police or Child Protective Services. She sat in her car wondering what she could do to make him back off from his apparent spying. It was the only way he could have known she'd left the girls alone to go to Club One. Or maybe he was having her trailed by a private eye. Whatever it was that he was doing, she knew she had to slow her activities a bit. "Not that he would ever take these girls home with him," she muttered angrily, then pulled away.

Back inside the office, Terryn dialed Nadia's number, barely able to wait for Nadia to answer. "Girrrrrrl." She spoke lowly, shifting her eyes left to ensure that no one was coming. "I told you Feenie had that man's kids."

"What are you talking about?"

"She just left here after she 'bout cussed Mr. Alexander out."

"You are too nosy. What'd they say?" Nadia dug while she eased her feet out of a pair of pumps and took a seat on her couch.

"He said something about her leaving his girls home by theirselves, and she was like *your* kids? *Your* kids?" Terryn exclaimed, recapping the story while she stooped to file away some court documents, completely unaware that Rance had walked around the corner and now stood at the receptionist desk. "He told her next time she left them he . . ." Terryn's heart practically stopped beating when she stood up to meet Rance's cold, hard stare. "Um . . . he told her next time to just leave the keys and he would have the car cleaned." She paused as if listening to a response from the other end of the phone. "Right. I told her that it would probably work better for her that way instead of her taking it to the dealer's."

"Someone must have walked up," Nadia discerned, noting the obvious switch in the conversation.

"Exactly. Listen, let me give you a call back, and I'll, um . . . I'll tell you when he picks the car up to wash it." Nervously she hung up the phone, avoiding eye contact with Rance and starting on a stack of letters that needed to be typed. "Did you need me to do something?" she offered, furrowing her brow, pretending to study her notes, which contained the details she needed for her letters.

"Actually, yes. I do need something. I need to see you in my office."

"Oh, sure. Just let me finish up—"

"Right now." His tone was calm but left no room for discussion or rebuttal. Terryn stood and followed Rance into his office. He sat at his desk and took his normal position of folding his fingers, then pressing them to his lips as he stared pensively.

"Yes, sir?"

"Were you just on a personal call?" he started.

"Uh . . . yes. I needed to call—"

"Whom were you speaking with?"

"A girlfriend of mine. Her boyfriend is supposed to be having her car washed," she lied.

"Her car washed?" he repeated as a question, raising a single brow. "So, what you are trying to convince me of is that I did not just overhear you sharing personal and confidential information?"

"I . . . I . . . I mean, I just was . . ." Terryn's sentence trailed off, then started again. "It probably sounded like I was talking about a client or something, but—"

"No, no. It wasn't a client you were talking about. I'm sure of that," Rance reassured her.

Terryn could think of no words, so she sat silent, feeling her heart pound inside her chest.

"Now, if I wanted to humor you, we could sit here and deliberate on what you were talking about, but I don't have time for that."

After a few seconds of quiet tension, Terryn spoke with a low volume. "It won't happen again, sir."

"Truer words have never been spoken," Rance responded in a tone so even and calm his fury couldn't be detected. "You need to get your things and leave. With no plans to come back here tomorrow, or any other day. Your last check will be mailed." There was nothing Terryn could say. She sat for a few seconds trying to gather her thoughts, trying to come up with a response that might save her job. As a paralegal, she made close to fifty thousand a year, and lived every dollar of it from paycheck to paycheck. She couldn't afford to be without a job.

"I'm sorry, Mr. Alexander. Is there anything—

I mean, I will never do this again if you give me another chance. I swear."

"You're fired." Rance still didn't change his tone or expression, which was completely stoic. Terryn bit her bottom lip as tears began to trickle down her face. "I'll see you to the door," he finished, rising to his feet. He waited for her to stand, then followed her to the front desk, watched as she lifted her purse from a file cabinet drawer, then collected a few pictures held on the wall with push pins. Without another word being spoken, he pushed the front door open and allowed her to pass before him.

Feeling like a fool, Terryn trod to her car, thinking over what had just happened, wishing she could turn back the hands of time. Why had she been so anxious to tell what she knew? Something that didn't even matter at that. So what if he'd cheated on his wife and had other kids? What concern was it of hers? On her drive home, her mind was flooded with a hundred similar questions. Included in them was how she was going to pay her rent and car note. There were only a few dollars in her checking account, and rent was due at the end of next week, and unfortunately, her last paycheck would only be a half day's pay, seeing as how she didn't even work the full day for being fired. She'd planned on using that check to make her rent payment, but now didn't know what she was going to do.

She cursed at herself as she pulled into her parking space at her eight-story apartment building. Stepping out of her BMW, she wondered how long she'd be able to hold on to it before the payments took her over.

"Don't think like that. I can find a new job," she coached herself, although she wasn't quite convinced. Working for Rance was the only job she'd ever had, and using him for a reference, or even risking putting his law firm on her résumé, was out of the question.

Pulling out her cell phone, she texted Nadia.

I got fired
What???? 4 what?
My boss hurd me talking 2 U 2day
O no! RU ok?
No—don't no how I will pay bills
Im sorry . . . do u want me 2 come over?
no, that's ok . . . need 2 start looking for a job
let me no if u need 2 talk
ok. I might need 2 come live with you! lol

Terryn closed her phone, took a shower, and went to bed although it was barely past twelve noon. But even in her sleep, she couldn't escape from the consequences of her choices, dreaming over and over, in different settings and scenes, of Rance firing her.

Four hours had passed since she'd lost her job. Now up again, Terryn sat at her computer trying to come up with a game plan. With her lips folded inside her mouth, her eyes floated around her sunroom and then into her living room, landing on her various belongings—things that she would probably have to pack up. A flat-screen television, a surround-sound speaker system, wall paintings, a white leather sectional with intricately carved tables, stacks of DVDs, books, a thirty-gallon tank of exotic fish, and several photos in elaborate frames. From where she sat, she focused on a picture she and Nadia had taken a few years back in Montego Bay. Clad in two-piece bathing suits, they both were kneeling in the wet sand where the waves had seconds before receded. She snickered a bit, remembering how they'd both said they were going to submit their photos to *Jet* magazine to be considered as a featured Beauty of the Week.

Her lips twisted a bit as she thought back on that one-week vacation. Terryn recalled having to save for months in order to make the trip, while all Nadia had to do was call her father. She thought even further back to their college years and how Nadia seemed never to struggle with needing books and not being able to pay for them, having to drop a class because her financial aid didn't come through, or having to survive on eight-packages-for-a-dollar noodles. Aidan had equipped Nadia with a car and a bank account, which he replenished every time Nadia rang his phone. *What gives Nadia the right to have things so easy?* she thought. A twinge of envy crept up her spine. She wished there was someone in her life that she could just call on the phone who would resolve all her financial woes. "Must be awfully nice," she commented aloud, "with her spoiled self."

As if she could hear Terryn commenting about her, Nadia called. "Are you okay?" she asked with sincere compassion.

"I'm going to be okay—there's no other way to

be. Call your daddy and ask him to let me borrow a couple thousand dollars."

"I wish it were that easy, girl. My daddy don't play when it comes to money."

Yeah, right, Terryn kept to herself.

"Do you need some company?"

"Mmmm," she thought momentarily. She started to decline, but from out of nowhere a wheel began spinning in her mind. "Yeah. Nothing like a good friend with some free Chinese food to cheer you up when you just lost your job," Terryn snickered.

"So I'll be there in, say—forty-five minutes?"

"Cool. Thanks, Nadia."

"That's what friends are for. What do you want to eat?"

"Some shrimp-fried rice, an order of chicken wings, some crab Rangoon with sweet and sour sauce, and two egg rolls."

"Deg, girl! Did you lose your job or find out you were pregnant?" Nadia exclaimed. "That's about twenty dollars' worth of food!"

"You know how we do when we're depressed . . . it's either shop or eat and we both know I'm not in a position to shop right now."

Within the hour, Nadia arrived with a grocery bagful of Asian cuisine and a DVD—*Stranger Than Fiction,* staring Will Ferrell and Queen Latifah.

"Thanks for coming, girl." Terryn sat Indian-style in front of her coffee table while Nadia curled into a corner of her couch, both with paper plates piled high with food.

"No problem. Hold on—don't start the movie until I get back." Nadia placed her plate on the end table, then scooted down the hall to the bathroom. As soon as Terryn heard the door shut, she quickly and quietly rose to her feet and peeked into Nadia's purse. In a matter of seconds she located her wallet and scanned it, hoping there would be some cash inside that she could ask for. Skillfully, she slid a nail between every crevice looking for gas money. In an outer zippered compartment, she smiled at several folded bills stuffed inside. Satisfied, she eased the wallet back into the purse and thought of a few ways to ask her for money that she didn't want to have to pay back. She slinked back to her original position and began digging into her meal. "You need some help back there?" she yelled down the hallway.

Nadia opened the bathroom door. "I'm coming; can I wash my hands first?" She returned to her seat, her plate, and the movie without a thought that her purse and wallet had been examined.

Right after the movie's end, Terryn formed the words to ask Nadia for one hundred dollars. She noticed Nadia's slight hesitation, but didn't let it bother her.

"This night has been expensive," Nadia commented, digging in her purse for her wallet. "And I don't even have a new pair of shoes to show for it."

"I really appreciate it, Nadia. You just don't know."

Nadia laid the bills in Terryn's hand, gave her a hug, and saw herself out. Terryn smiled smugly to herself. She didn't feel the least bit guilty knowing that Nadia had access to cash at the snap of a finger even if she didn't ask Aidan for money on her behalf. *There's more than one way to skin a cat*, she thought to herself as she took a seat in front of her computer.

She spent the next hour visiting job posting boards, finding nothing that would match her previous salary, or would take her with no experience, although she had five years' worth. She became distracted and discouraged, and the more discouraged she became, the more her anger against Rance increased, although in her heart she knew she couldn't be angry at anyone besides herself. She found her fingers typing in the word *blackmail*.

CHAPTER 12

It was like clockwork. Every evening around the same time, Feenie went switching her hot hips over to Jonathan's door carrying a plate of something. And every night, he let her in for at least five minutes, but tonight she was on extended stay. Five minutes turned into ten, which turned into fifteen, which turned into twenty. Finally at the twenty-two-and-a-half mark, she came out again, pulling down her shirt. Ooh, she made Nadia sick! Now, normally Nadia didn't compete for a man, but this time she was determined that she wouldn't let Feenie win. What had she been doing over there all that time? Maybe they'd sat down and eaten and laughed and talked like she and Jonathan were supposed to do the other night before he practically stormed out. Or maybe he was getting some extended use out of his size larges. And now that Nadia was thinking about it, she realized that when she'd mentioned Feenie the other night, Jonathan didn't actually deny it. He just laughed it off. *That was probably a trick to make me think that him seeing her was just beyond ridiculous.* Trickery at its finest!

But then again, maybe not. After all, he did e-mail Nadia and apologize. That had to be worth something. And if Nadia was completely honest with herself, she did have some interest in Jonathan, but wasn't sure if it was safe to show, especially since he seemed to be entertaining Feenie so much. Although Nadia was confident that Feenie couldn't hold a candle to her, she wanted to keep Jonathan guessing about her interest, so she hid it as much as she could. Even when he came tapping at her door out of the clear blue sky after letting Feenie out. Of course Nadia had pulled away from the window and wasn't expecting anyone, so she had been just sitting around in her panties and oversized T-shirt, watching old episodes of *Girlfriends* on DVD and painting her toenails.

"Who is it?" she yelled from the couch when he knocked.

"Jonathan."

As usual, her eyes raced around the room, instinctively scanning for how neat or junky the living room was. "Just a minute," she yelled, scooting to her bedroom with a stack of magazines, a pair of socks, and a bag from Wal-Mart filled with feminine hygiene products. From her bedroom, she hopped to the front door trying to get her foot through the leg of a pair of sweats. Right before she opened the door, she blew her breath into her palm, decided on a piece of gum, ran a hand across her hair, then pulled the door back.

"Hey. What's going on?"

"Nothing." He shrugged. "Just came over to see what you were up to." He had a box tucked under his arm, but Nadia didn't study it.

"Just painting my toes and watching TV. Where's Pazzo?" Nadia casually turned away, leaving the door open so he could come in, and he did.

"At the house. Sometimes I need some real company, you know?"

"Yeah. Have a seat," she offered, patting the red microsuede sofa she'd purchased a few days ago from Ikea.

"Thank you. I brought Scrabble," he sang, revealing the box he'd brought in with him while his eyes roamed her body for a flash of a second. "Wanna play?" He caught her blushing.

"Sure. I gotta warn you, though; I'ma beat you like you stole something."

"We'll see." He repositioned a set of tea light candles, pushing them one at a time to the table's edge along with a bottle of nail polish remover.

"Want something to drink?" Nadia asked, rising to her feet and taking an empty wineglass to the kitchen for a partial refill. "I have some white peach wine."

He turned the corners of his mouth down pensively. "That sounds good. Sounds like a girl wine, though."

"Well, last I checked I'm not a boy." Nadia added a little twist to her hips to let him know that she was all woman.

"You're right about that," she heard him mumble under his breath, but didn't acknowledge. She half filled their glasses, grabbed a box of Wheat Thins, and sauntered back to the living room. Jonathan had the board set up and was flipping tiles over to the blank sides in preparation of a little friendly competition. "So, how was your day today?"

"It was pretty uneventful. Nothing to write home about. Typical day. How about you? Did you close any super global accounts this afternoon?"

"Not exactly," he answered, raising his eyebrows while he reached up to scratch his head. "It was a pretty typical day for me as well."

Nadia bobbed her head as she selected tiles and added them to her rack.

"You're cheating already, huh?"

"What do you mean? I don't have to cheat you to beat you."

"You're supposed to flip a tile to see who goes first, cheater," he teased.

"Oh yeah! I forgot all about that!"

"Yeah, right." He smirked. "I'll just let you go first," he said, randomly picking seven squares.

Rearranging her letters, Nadia formed the word *clean* on her rack, disappointed that it would only net twenty points, but placed it on the board anyway as she pondered asking him about Feenie.

"That's the best you can do?" he chuckled, privately switching letters around. "This is gonna be easy."

Not intimidated, Nadia swallowed a mouthful of wine, then let the words pass through her lips. "So, what's up with you and ol' girl?"

"Who is that?" he asked, never looking up. Using the *n* from Nadia's word, he added letters to make the word *sprinkle*, scoring a whopping sixty-five points since he'd used all seven of his letters in one play. He smiled smugly, proud of himself. "Who're you talking about?"

"Feenie," she said, lifting her glass to her mouth a second time to hide any emotion that threatened to show through on her face other than a slightly raised eyebrow. He guffawed.

"What made you ask about her?"

Nadia immediately recognized his question avoidance and quickly summed up there was definitely something up between them. She paused long enough to put *carpet* on the board.

"I know she likes you. She's not tipping over there with dinner just for something to do." Nadia's hand slid into the open box of crackers and stuffed one in her mouth as she waited for Jonathan's response.

"Please. She's just getting rid of leftovers."

Mmm-hmm. Likely story, Nadia thought.

"Is she a good cook?" she probed further, hoping he would slip up and say something incriminating.

"I have no idea," he said nonchalantly as he placed more tiles on the board, then jotted down his score.

"What do you mean you have no idea? She brings you dinner just about every night."

He shot his eyes toward Nadia and she easily read their message, which was *how do you know?* Nadia silently reprimanded herself, figuring that she needed to eat more crackers and talk a little less.

"No, she doesn't." His tone was flat but defensive, so Nadia left it alone, but made a mental note of it. Their next couple of turns were silent until Nadia added a seven-letter word on the board.

"That's what I'm talking about," he said, impressed. "Give me a little bit of a challenge."

"You didn't think I was going to just let you win, did you?"

Jonathan didn't answer. He studied his tiles for a few seconds before he spoke again.

"I don't eat that food that she brings over," he said just before he gulped down some wine.

"What do you do with it, then? Give it to Pazzo?"

"Heck no!" he said, crinkling his brows, clearly offended that Nadia could ever think such a thing. "I throw it in the trash."

"Deg!" she giggled. "Thanks for telling me. I know now not to ever cook you anything!"

"Please don't tell her that." He chuckled a little himself.

"You don't have to worry about that; we don't talk. I meant to tell you she . . ." She had to stop herself in her tracks because she was about to tell on herself.

"She what?"

"She, um . . . she saw me walking Pazzo and asked me when you were going to be home," Nadia made up on the fly. "With her nosy self."

"What did you tell her?" Before she could answer he cut her off. "What in the world is that word?" Nadia had spelled out the word *prink*. "That is not a word."

"Yes, it is," she insisted.

"Use it in a sentence."

"Feenie loves to prink around thinking she's cute and trying to get your attention."

Jonathan burst out in laughter.

"Get the dictionary," he challenged. "That wine has gone to your head."

"You don't believe me?" Nadia leapt to her feet and headed to her bookshelf.

"Prink is not a word," he laughed.

Much to her surprise, Jonathan followed closely behind.

"Don't be tryna look at my letters!" she shrieked, darting back to the table to turn her letters down. In her haste, she tripped on Jonathan's foot and by natural reflex he wrapped his arms around her to save her from a fall. And while it was only a few seconds before he released her, the strength of his hands circling her waist felt mighty good.

"Be careful," he said, steadying Nadia on her feet.

Man! She didn't want him to let her go, but he did. Nadia recovered and grabbed the dictionary; then they both sat down again. And just like that, things were back to normal.

"Let me see if you know what you're talking about." He took the book from Nadia's hand and thumbed through while she sat back confidently, again sipping from her glass. A few seconds later with twisted lips, Jonathan dropped the book on the table and gave himself a zero. "So, Feenie prinks, huh?"

"Yep! She be prinkin'."

Jonathan chuckled out loud as he recorded Nadia's score.

"Really. There's nothing to that," he added, finally answering her questions with a shake of his head. "She does come over trying to feed me, but I'm not interested in her." He looked up at Nadia, who searched his eyes for sincerity. She didn't know if she saw it, but she did notice that his eyes were a beautiful shade of brown. They weren't light brown, like contacts, but not as dark as the average brown African-American eye color. It was something in between. Nadia started to compliment him, but quickly thought better of it, thinking he'd probably heard how beautiful his eyes were a million times before.

"What's the score?" she asked as a distraction tactic.

He glanced down at the score sheet. "You're leading by twenty-two points."

"Yeah!" Nadia shot to her feet again and started pop-locking in celebration.

"Don't get too happy; the game's not over yet," he said, placing tiles on the board in an effort to catch up. Before Nadia could finish her happy dance, the phone rang.

"Excuse me while I get that." Glancing at the caller ID, she saw it was a number she didn't recognize. "Hello?"

"Hey, Nadia!" a woman's voice said, assuming familiarity.

"Hey," she answered instinctively but puzzled as to who it was.

"Girl, I'm glad I caught you; it's Michelle."

"Who?" Nadia didn't know any Michelles off the top of her head. Still on the phone, she eyed Jonathan, who was studying how he could take advantage of a triple-letter premium space.

"Michelle," she repeated in a tone that suggested she should easily have recognized her name or voice. "Listen, I was just looking over your account and noticed that you haven't made a payment to your Visa in months. I was calling to see how I could help you out with that."

"What?"

"Yeah, we were expecting a payment of two hundred and seventeen dollars every month, but since you haven't made one, that total amount past due is now eight hundred and sixty-eight dollars and I wanted to see what I could do to help you get that current."

"I don't know who your are; I think you have the wrong number," Nadia said, choosing her words carefully, not wanting to give Jonathan an idea of what the phone call was about.

"Um, no. This is . . ."

Truly puzzled, Nadia struggled between hearing more of what Michelle had to say and just hanging up after seeing Jonathan shoot his eyes her way for a split second. Although she knew that she didn't owe anyone, she felt a surge of embarrassment knowing the perception that he could be forming.

"Yeah, that's my number, but I'm still not certain you're calling the right number, because I don't know what you're talking about and I have company right now." Nadia hung up the phone before Michelle could squeeze in another word. Jonathan seemed not to be listening, but Nadia knew he couldn't help but overhear since she was standing only a few feet away. She had only taken two steps to rejoin him before the phone rang again. Nadia looked at the number thinking it was Michelle calling back a second time but broke into a smile when she recognized her father's phone number on the display. She answered without hesitation.

"Hey, Daddy,"

"Hey, baby girl. How are you doing?"

"Good. Just in here beating my neighbor at a game of Scrabble."

"So you have company."

"Yes," she sang. "So I can't talk long, Daddy. You and Mama always taught me that that was rude."

"Yeah, it is. Is it a gentleman caller?"

"Mmm-hmm."

"The bracelet guy?"

"Yep."

"Is he acting right?"

"Of course."

"He's respecting you?"

"Or else he wouldn't be here."

"All right. Call me later, baby girl, somebody just called here looking for you, talking about some owed money."

"Huh?" She crinkled her brow, perplexed. Nadia always paid her bills on time—even if she had to use Aidan's money to do it. And Aidan McKenzie Mitchell wouldn't have it any other way.

"Just call me when your company leaves and let me know what's going on."

"I will, Daddy," she promised. "Love you."

"Love you too."

"So, you're a daddy's-girl, huh?" Jonathan piped in right away.

"A little bit," she easily admitted, wanting to tag on that she knew he was a mama's boy judging from the journal entry she'd read at his house. Instead she filled her mouth with more crackers to keep her mouth shut and plopped down on the couch again, then spelled out her next word.

"Where do your parents live?" he asked.

"My dad lives in South Carolina and my mom in Vegas."

"So, when do I get to meet your parents?" he asked without looking up.

"The same day that I meet your mama, I guess," she answered, trying to be funny.

"I'm glad you said that, because I was trying to think of a way to ask you if you wanted to come home with me."

What? With her brow furrowed and her lips puckered, Nadia felt like saying, "Whatchu talkin' 'bout, Willis?" a line made famous by Gary Coleman's character, Arnold, from the sitcom *Different Strokes.* "Are you serious?"

"Yeah. I am."

"But I mean . . . I just . . . I thought . . ." What did she think? Nadia didn't know what to think. Or say, for that matter. He wanted her to go home with him to meet his mama? He was submitting her for approval!

"It's no big deal if you don't want to go." He shrugged. "Just thought you might be interested in a little getaway."

"When are you trying to go?"

"Probably Labor Day weekend."

"And you want me to go with you?" she asked with skepticism.

"Sometimes I get a little bored traveling by

myself. After a while a laptop and a few books and magazines just don't cut it anymore."

"So you just want me to keep you company on your plane ride?" she asked, seeking clarification, hoping that it was really more.

"If you're looking for something to do that weekend."

Nadia couldn't help but think about the note that she'd found from Feenie. "Let me get back to you." He sighed, but so what? He wasn't all that, Nadia reasoned. Well, yes, he was, but she wasn't going to tell him. Plus, she needed to think about whether she wanted to put herself through Ms. Lola Strickland's eye of scrutiny, knowing that no woman before her had ever passed.

That Friday at seven o'clock on the dot, Jonathan rang Nadia's doorbell. Since she hadn't had a chance to wear the dress she'd spent so much money on the other week, and tonight was a special occasion, Nadia thought she'd sport it. Her jaw almost hit the floor when she opened her door and saw Jonathan standing there in a pair of faded jeans, a basic gray T-shirt, and what Nadia called man sandals, the wide leather kind that let the toes peek out a bit with no backs around the heel.

While his eyes seemed to appreciate the tight black calf-length dress Nadia wore, accented with silver loopy jewelry and black shoes with a silver stiletto heel, his mouth said, "You might want to change clothes." Immediately she was heated but did her best not to show it and take it all in stride.

Okay, so it's a little much for Applebee's, but I can rock it. "No, I'm fine like this," Nadia insisted.

"Okay," he sang, raising his eyebrows in a have-it-your-way kind of look.

"Let me just grab my purse and keys." Nadia walked through the living room to her sofa table and grabbed a small black resin clutch. "I'm ready. Where are we going?"

"To one of my favorite places." He opened the car door for her, then walked around to his side, took his seat, and backed out of the driveway. Visions of Outback Steakhouse began to dance around in Nadia's head. They had a few new things on their menu that she wanted to try. If they weren't going there, Nadia figured it wouldn't be too far off—surely Applebee's was far from a favorite place.

She struggled to hide her disappointment when Jonathan drove across town and pulled onto the road that led into Patterson Park. *Patterson Park! I'm looking all sexy in this expensive-tail dress and hot stilettos! I'm too fine to be sitting in the midst of some grass, trees, and tennis courts!*

Jonathan parked, walked around to the passenger side, and opened the door for Nadia. Taking her by the hand, he grabbed a basket out of the trunk and led her down a sidewalk to a shelter with a couple of picnic tables. Once they got there, he took out a classic red and white tablecloth (made of paper, Nadia noted) and spread it out on the table. Then he reached into the basket and pulled out a Chick-Fil-a bag. *What the sam hill!* Nadia thought, becoming so angry she started to laugh out loud. *This man is going to serve me some cold waffle fries and a smashed-up chicken sandwich. I played hard to get for this? And he got the nerve to be smiling like he's really showing me something. Wait till I tell my daddy!*

Jonathan sat beside Nadia and they ate in silence until Jonathan spoke a few words. "I love it out here."

Nadia didn't respond, silently fuming. *What? It's about ninety degrees outside, I'm sitting here swatting at mosquitoes, stomping ants, diving bees, and shooing flies. What is there to love about this? Especially when I'm dressed to the nines. This absolutely sucks.*

CHAPTER 13

Jonathan found himself looking out of his living room window. Usually by now Feenie would have knocked on the door. He wasn't even interested in eating her prepared meals, but looked for her nonetheless, out of habit, he told himself. Yet he wondered why she hadn't come.

"I could use a good home-cooked meal right now," he said to Pazzo. Pazzo trotted over, jumped up on the couch, and practically lay in his master's lap, while Jonathan picked up the phone to call Lola. "Hey, Ma," he started once she answered.

"Hey, handsome. You all right?"

"I'm just fine. Just missing you and your cooking."

"Well, that means I'ma have to come out there and cook my baby boy something to eat. When you want me to come?"

"In a few weeks, I guess. I have someone I need you to meet."

"Boy, I thought you wanted to see me. You got a motive."

"I do want to see you, Ma, but I also want you

to take a look at this woman that lives across the street."

"What she do for a living? She got a job?"

"Of course."

"Doing what?"

"She works in management development doing corporate training."

"Can she cook?"

"Ma, there's more to life than rattling pots and pans."

"Yeah, but if she cain't do that, you ain't gone have no life, 'cause you gone starve to death."

"I haven't starved yet."

"You don't want no woman who cain't cook, Jonathan. I'm telling you what I know."

"Yes, ma'am," he answered, giving in.

"She got kids?"

"No. Come on, Ma, I have the basics covered. She's a good girl," he said assuredly.

"Mm-hmm. I'll see when I get out there. What kind of bills she got? She ain't tryna get you to pay her bills, is she?"

Jonathan had to pause as he remembered the portion of the phone call he'd overheard while at Nadia's house. He was convinced it had been a bill collector's call. "I don't know to be honest with you, Ma, we've not gotten that far in our discussions. I need you to meet her first. And you know what else I need?" he asked, shifting the discussion.

"What's that?"

"I need you to make me some meat loaf, lasagna, macaroni and cheese, seven-layer salad, fry me some chicken, bake a turkey with homemade dressing, I could use some cabbage in my life, and some yeast rolls."

"Just buy the stuff, baby, and I'll take care of it. How soon you gone send my ticket?"

"How about in a few weeks when I can take a little break from the office?"

"I guess I can pull myself together by then. I'll need to put a few things in the cleaners unless you giving me shopping money when I get there."

"How about you just give me your dry cleaning bill?" he chuckled.

"Okay. I got some other bills I need you to take a look at for me too." By "taking a look at," Lola meant "pay."

"What kind of bills, Ma?"

"Well, Dr. Pittman sent something here the other day for six hundred dollars for my last visit. Adonna opened me up a Target account the other day while we were in there picking up a few things for the baby. You know that baby ain't have nothing to wear?"

"A Target account?"

"Yeah. We were in there to get the baby some Pampers, and the girl asked us if we wanted to open an account and get ten percent off the stuff we were buying. I didn't think nothing of it, and Adonna said I should, so she went on and filled it out for me and it got approved right then and there," Lola explained.

"Ma, what in the world do you need with a Target account? How are you going to pay for it?"

"Well, I guess I didn't need it, but like I just told you, it's a good thing they went on and gave it to me because that baby girl of Adonna's didn't have a strip of clothes for the summer. She got that child running around in hot jeans and long-sleeve shirts that been cut off and rolled up, made to look like shorts and a T-shirt. I can't have my grandbaby out there looking like that."

"Where is Ashley's daddy, Ma? Adonna didn't have that child by herself, and I wasn't the one to help her make her—neither were you. Adonna needs to get her lazy behind up and get a job to support her own kids. Don't bring me that bill," he stated firmly.

"Well, I'll take care of the part that was for the clothes for the baby!" Lola snapped. "But it's a shame when you can't depend on your family to help you out when you're in a bind. As much as you hate it, Adonna, Stephanie, and Diane are my kids too! And just like I bent over backward to make sure you could get through school and have the things you needed, I'ma do that for my girls."

"There's nothing wrong with you doing that, Ma, if that is what you choose to do, but don't bring me the bill; why should I have to pay for it? Diane popping out babies like some kind of rabbit, Stephanie wasting her money on shopping sprees, and Adonna refusing to work or hold that man accountable to take care of his kids—and I'm supposed to help them?" Jonathan asked, becoming frustrated.

"Why wouldn't you help them? They're your sisters—you're supposed to love them," Lola shot back.

"I do love them, but that doesn't make me financially responsible for their lives."

"Boy, you done forgot where your little snotty

nose came from," Lola responded sharply. "You forgot about the time somebody had to see after you. Send their whole paycheck out there to Maryland so you could stay in school for one more semester. Eat noodles at home to make sure you weren't missing any meals out there. Work extra hours so you could have the books you needed. You done forgot all that, huh?"

"Ma, that was twelve years ago!"

"Who are you yelling at?" Lola barked, bringing Jonathan back in line. He inhaled as deeply as he could, then pushed the air out of his lips slowly before he started again.

"That was twelve years ago, Ma," he repeated. "I know you made sacrifices for me and I appreciate it so much. And I think I've shown my appreciation, and still do."

"Well, I sure can't tell. Every time I ask you for something you act like I'm asking for blood," she continued, her voice beginning to change octaves and tremble a bit.

Jonathan rolled his eyes, glad that she couldn't see him.

"I'm just trying to enjoy my life. I raised all four of you all by myself and never complained one day. Neither you nor your sisters have never missed a meal or went nowhere looking like orphans. Now, you might not have had the best, but I kept y'all clean, clothed, healthy, and fed. Not one time have I *ever* sent you to bed hungry. Even if it meant I had to be on a fast until some money came in from somewhere. Now that y'all done grown up, I guess it's asking too much to enjoy the fruits of my labor."

"Ma, please stop."

"Now, the Bible says in First Timothy, Thou shalt not muzzle the ox that treadeth out the corn. And the laborer is worthy of his reward. I done labored; I done treaded, and sowed, and tilled, and worked till the sun went down, but I guess I'm not supposed to reap the harvest. I tell you what, I'll just go ahead and keep these bills I got. Don't worry about it. The Lord will make a way somehow. He always does."

"Just bring them with you when you come, Ma."

Lola only sighed in response.

"Did you hear me?"

"Yeah, I heard you, son. I'll think about it," she answered, knowing full well every bill she had would be making the trip with her to Baltimore. "I just feel like I'm being a burden and I don't mean to be."

"You're not being a burden. You know I love you and would do anything for you."

"Well, thank you, Jonathan," she said meekly.

He rubbed his temples, now plagued with a headache. "So I'll see you in a few weeks?"

"I suppose you will."

"All right, Ma," he said, bringing the call to a close.

"I'll talk to you later. I need to go in here and take my pressure pills and lie down for a while. I'm feeling a little dizzy."

"Okay, Ma. Love you."

"Love you too, baby."

CHAPTER 14

It had been three weeks since Terryn had been dismissed from Rance's office, and she had yet to secure alternate employment. It wasn't that she hadn't been trying . . . at least a little. The first part of every day was spent on Careerbuilder.com seeking what new jobs had posted. And every day she'd sigh in frustration, realizing that she'd have to build her career from the bottom up all over again. There were no paralegal jobs that didn't require at least one year of experience, and most that only required minimal experience weren't paying what Terryn knew she needed and wanted to make. Although she'd posted for a few jobs, they weren't in her field and had menial pay, so her interest was nearly nonexistent.

She slid into a depressive funk, spending the rest of the day slouching around the house, doing nothing but feeling sorry for herself. Gas was too high to drive anywhere, other than to the mall, where she had a ton of store credit card accounts, so like days before, she showered, pulled on a pair of jeans, a camisole top, and a pair of heels to head for the mall for some shopping therapy. While she knew she couldn't afford to do much, even the purchase of one small thing would make her feel better. At least it was Saturday, a day made for shopping.

"Come go shopping with me," she said to Nadia after speed-dialing her number from her cell.

"I can't," Nadia whined.

"Yes, you can, come on. I need a shoulder to cry on and a partner to shop with."

"No, seriously, I can't. I'm broke, and my dad froze all my credit cards."

"Why?" Terryn asked, taken aback.

"Because first of all, I have no cash, and second, some lady has been calling claiming that I owe thousands of dollars for some Visa account, and until we figure out what's going on my dad won't let me buy anything. And you wouldn't want me around in the mall when I can't buy something."

"Wait a minute, though. What Visa account is she talking about?"

"I have no clue. They are supposed to be sending me a bill for this so-called account that was opened up in Texas somewhere. I've never even been to Texas, let alone lived there to open up somebody's account."

"Girl, that sounds like someone has stolen your identity," Terryn gasped. "You need to pull your credit report and see what is up there."

"I know. I feel so violated! How is somebody going to take my information and charge a ton of debt to me!"

"What are you going to do about it?"

"I have no idea where to start, other than them

sending me some statements and stuff. And I just don't understand how the account was opened in Texas, but the phone number they have for me is my number here in Maryland," Nadia ranted.

"Did you lose your wallet or anything?"

"No. I haven't lost anything, I haven't been anywhere, I haven't done anything."

"Do you shop online? Because you know that has happened to a lot of people who put their personal information out there on those unsecured Web sites," Terryn offered, trying to help Nadia think of how this could have happened to her.

"No—I mean, I shop online, but you know I'm pretty careful about where and how I shop. I just don't be putting my information on any old site."

"I'm so sorry you going through this, girl. I still say a little shopping is just what you need."

"I would, but I'm broke as . . . as a vase of roses being thown out of a third-floor apartment window after a girl has found out her man has cheated on her."

"That's pretty broke," Terryn giggled. "But you're not alone. I'm broke right with you, and still looking for a job, but at least I still have my accounts to ease me through my pain."

"Lucky you."

"You should at least let me buy you lunch. I owe you from the Chinese food you brought over the other night. We can just grab something at the food court. And if I see something cute for cheap, I can pick it up for you—I got room on my credit card." She paused to allow Nadia to answer. "Please!" Terryn whined. "I really need some girlfriend time."

"All right. Let me put something on and meet you out there. You better keep me away from my favorite stores, though."

"Deal!"

Within the hour Nadia and Terryn were strolling from store to store at the Gallery at Harborplace as if their purses were full of cash, stopping in various stores and picking up an item or two. Once they reached the food court, they chose to take a break to grab lunch. Deciding on Sbarro Italian Eatery, Terryn ordered rigatoni à la vodka, a pasta dish topped with the restaurant's special vodka sauce, romano cheese, bacon, and parsley, along with a Caesar salad, bread sticks, and sweet tea, while Nadia chose two thick slices of pizza featuring fresh sautéed spinach, yellow peppers, mozzarella cheese, and a savory sauce, and layers of chocolate sponge cake with a rich cherry center, covered with buttercream icing and topped with a buttercream rosette and a cherry, along with a Pepsi.

Terryn gawked at her choices. "Girl, keep it up; you're gonna start saying ba-deh bah-deh ba-deh, that's all, folks!" she laughed, mocking Looney Tunes' Porky Pig.

"Shut up." Nadia smacked her teeth. "I've been eating peanut butter and jelly all week, I can afford a few extra calories," she finished as they took their seats. "So, what are you going to do about work?"

Terryn shrugged. "I'm looking but not finding anything," she answered, shaking her head before inserting a forkful of pasta into her mouth and chewing deliberately. "Seriously, I might need to come stay with you for a little while," she added, avoiding eye contact, pretending to be more interested in her meal.

"Are you for real?"

"Yeah. I don't have the money to pay my rent, which is already seven weeks behind because I didn't pay it last month like I was supposed to." This time she did look into her friend's face.

"Well . . ." Nadia stalled a bit, which Terryn sensed but was desperate for help. "I do have an extra bedroom. How soon do you need to move in?"

"Pretty much right now. I'm already behind for last month, and next month starts next week, and I haven't put in my thirty days' notice, so I'm about to be owing them about four thousand dollars."

"I don't see why in the world you just didn't buy a house with all that money you were making," Nadia commented, biting into her veggie pizza.

"Not with my jacked-up credit. I owe some of everybody. I can't remember the last time I was actually able to enjoy my paycheck."

Nadia frowned, realizing that Terryn would want to stay in her home rent free. "How long do you think you will need to stay?"

"Maybe just for a couple of months. I'm sure I be back working soon."

"Yeah, but if you give your place up, how are you going to find another apartment? Especially if your credit is not up to par."

"There's always somebody somewhere needing to rent a house. They can't all say no, can they? I know plenty of people with bad credit that find places to live all the time. I didn't tell you that a deposition came in the other day for Nicole Manning getting evicted out of her place; remember her?"

"Not really," Nadia replied, not caring about whoever Nicole was, but thinking more about how she could help Terryn short term only.

"She was that skank that tried to break me and Keshawn up that time," Terryn reminded her. "Girl, if I knew then what I later found out, I would have quickly surrendered his cheating behind. One thing I can't stand is a cheating man!" Terryn's thoughts went from her former fiancé, Keshawn, and his sexcapades to what she knew about Rance and Feenie. "That's why I can't stand Mr. Alexander," she said, still faulting him for her own misfortune.

"Terryn, seriously, you did that to yourself. I told you to stay out of people's business."

"Okay, Miss 'I'm going to snoop around Jonathan's house just to see what I can find.'"

"Well, at least I had the sense enough not to get caught."

"You don't know what kind of cameras that man might have set up in his house," Terryn shot. "I mean, he only been knowing you for a few months. Would you seriously trust someone in your house and you were just really getting to know them?" Terryn stood, taking her meal remnants to the trash can, followed by Nadia.

"Well, I'm a woman, so it's different for me. You know guys don't care about that kind of stuff," Nadia replied, hoping that there were no secret surveillance cameras in Jonathan's home.

"Yeah, keep thinking that. He probably knows

you been all in his stuff. Did you see if any matchsticks fell off the top of any doors?"

"What?" Nadia dumped her tray and the ladies headed toward their next shopping destination.

"You know how old folks used to close a match or something in the door to be able to tell if the door had been opened?"

"I've never heard of that. That's some old-school trickery right there."

"Well, you better hope you ain't fall in the nosy trap like I did. Let's go in here right quick." Terryn pulled Nadia into a gift shop. "I need to get an anniversary card for my grandparents." Rhianna's "Take a Bow" was playing through the store's speakers, which Terryn immediately started to sing as she again thought about all the cheaters she knew, and how she could get back at them, specifically Rance Alexander. Leaving Nadia in the birthday card section, she wandered down the next aisle to a section of blank cards, looking at image after image until she found a few perfectly suited for what she wanted to do. A black-and-white image of a woman pressing a single finger to her lips, an image of a black woman's hand interlaced with that of a white man's, and one of a white couple tightly wound in each other's embrace. She picked two of each card, paid for her merchandise, and slid the flat bag into her purse.

"I'm ready when you are," she announced. "What are you looking at?"

"Nothing," Nadia lied, slipping a thank-you card back in its slot. She had actually been thinking of giving Jonathan a card to thank him for their outing although it was far beneath what she'd expected. The only reason she remotely considered it was that she thought it might gain her a point or two if he was on the cusp of trying to decide if he wanted to date her or not. "Let's go."

After hitting a few more stores, and purchasing a "gotta have 'em" pair of jeans from Bebe for Nadia, the ladies went their separate ways. Terryn was more than anxious to get home to begin devising her plan to have Rance pay what was soon to be her back rent.

Taking a seat at her desk, she pulled out a sheet of paper and jotted down what she thought she would need: greeting cards, several magazines to cut out words from, a glue stick, tweezers, scissors, rubber gloves, a few pictures of Feenie, a few pictures of Rance, and a few of the twins, stamps, envelopes, and a bank account that couldn't be traced back to her. That would be the tricky part. Other than that she had all of the items in her home already, including a box of gloves, which she used to apply relaxers to her hair. All she needed was to set up a bank account, and she planned to do that online tomorrow at the local library, rather than from her home computer. On another sheet of paper, Terryn began composing a letter to Rance, which she would later use to find the words in magazines to piece together.

> *I know a secret. I know your secret. I'm not good at keeping secrets, but you can help me to keep yours. Deposit $2,000 into this account ———— every Friday, beginning September 3, and your secret will be safe with me. I'll make sure your wife doesn't know. Shhh!*

Once Terryn set up the account, she would include the account number, and also planned to include photos of Feenie and the girls.

"Maybe I won't have to stay with Nadia too long after all."

After enjoying a cup of coffee and a cinnamon bagel with cream cheese at Panera Bread, Terryn headed for the library that next afternoon. Using just her initials, she signed into the computer use log and took a seat at a free workstation. Logging on to WaMu.com, she quickly filled in information to set up a new checking account that she could easily access and monitor online. Within seven minutes, she was provided with a routing and account number to finish off her plan. Just for appearance's sake, Terryn browsed other sites, watched YouTube videos, and played a few online games until a complete hour passed. She then headed home to start cutting and pasting her first letter.

CHAPTER 15

For the next two weeks, Feenie didn't let the girls out of her sight, scared that Rance might be lurking around the corner with Child Protective Services on speed dial. She felt like Mary with some little lambs, because everywhere she went, the twins were sure to go, and Feenie was sure to look over her shoulder every step of the way. Her attitude about actually taking the kids everywhere with her was apparent. Most days her face was balled into a tight knot, and her eyes rolled more than a bucket of marbles dumped on the toy aisle of a department store. She strictly forbade the girls to call Rance at all, blocking his number from being dialed from her home, and blocking his from coming in.

Even though she felt the girls' constant presence impacted her personal life far more than she liked, she focused all her energy on spending time with her daughters; just in case anyone came knocking on the door, she wanted the girls to have only good things to say. For twenty-one days straight, she made the girls breakfast, read them books, took them to the library, caught a few movies, did some shopping, and even took them up to Pennsylvania to go to Sesame Place—all the while, her face filled with disdain.

"Mommy sure is being real nice to us all of a sudden," Mia whispered during one of the girls' private bedtime discussions.

"I know."

"I wonder why."

"I don't know. I still wanna go live with Daddy, though," Cara said.

"For real?"

"Yep."

"You gonna call him?" Mia whispered even lower.

"I'ma try to. The last time I tried to call him, it didn't work, though."

"Maybe he got his phone cut off."

"I can try again tomorrow."

"You think he's gonna let us come live with him?"

"I don't know. I think he will."

"Me too."

Feenie listened quietly right outside their bedroom door. She wanted to burst in and harshly reprimand them, but didn't want it to get back to Rance, somehow. Once the girls changed the subject she tiptoed to her bedroom and shut the door.

"Thank you so much for letting me come stay." Terryn heaved the last box of her limited belongings out of her trunk and slid them to a corner of Nadia's garage. "I really do appreciate it."

"No problem. That's what friends are for. You do know it's your night to wash the dishes, right?"

"What? I haven't even eaten yet!"

"Sorry, house rules. The last one to move in has to wash the dishes on their first night of stay," Nadia snickered.

"Whatever." Terryn lifted her laptop bag and a large tote bag from the passenger seat. "Show me to my room please."

"Right this way, ma'am." Nadia led the way up a few stairs and through the door into the kitchen. "You know where it is. I'm going to start on dinner; guess who's coming over?" She pulled open a kitchen drawer that was full of menus.

"Who, Supersonic?" Nadia laughed out loud at the nickname Terryn had given Jonathan based upon his large paycheck and large condoms.

"Him *and* his mama."

"What? You're meeting the mama?"

Nadia nodded with pressed lips and raised brows.

"What are you going to cook?"

"Cook? Girl, please, I'm about to order some food from Red, Hot, and Blue and put that mess in some serving dishes."

"I heard that! I'll be in here putting away a few things."

"Make yourself at home." A few minutes later, Nadia had placed an order for wet ribs, two Memphis half chickens, potato salad, baked beans, green beans, and hush puppies. After a quick shower, she headed out to pick up her "home-cooked" meal. "Be right back!" she yelled before sliding out.

Terryn used the time that Nadia was away to do more cutting and pasting for her blackmail attempt, knowing she would have to secretly manage it so Nadia wouldn't find out. It was tedious work searching for words in different fonts, but she couldn't risk any letters being mistakenly stored on any computer. With gloved hands, she carefully cut out words and placed them in an envelope, then marked them off her words-needed list. She still had five days before the first letter needed to be put in the mail, and she had yet to get a photo of Feenie and the girls. Hearing Nadia's Honda Accord pull up in the driveway, Terryn quickly put her things away, inserted the envelope into a folder and slid it back into her laptop bag. She scooted out of the front door to help Nadia bring the food inside.

"Did you need me to leave during your dinner? I got a few errands to run anyway."

"You don't have to; you're welcome to stay, especially since you gotta wash the dishes."

"Oh, I *know* I'm getting up outta here now!" she laughed. "But I'll help you get the food straight first," she offered.

As planned, Nadia was comfortably but impressively dressed and had dinner on the table in time for Jonathan and Lola's visit. She used the few extra minutes she had to rearrange her hair in a style that was subtly sexy. Just as the doorbell rang, she checked her appearance one last time, turning to make sure her panties weren't visible through the white capris she wore, and tugged at her red knit sleeveless top.

She opened the door to find Jonathan proudly

standing behind a woman dressed in a coral linen pantsuit with a bright smile and a critical eye.

"Hello! You must be Jonathan's mother; I'm Nadia."

"Hi, shug," she greeted. "Nice to meet you."

"Come on in. Hi, Jonathan," she squeezed in.

"Hey, Nadia."

Lola wasted no time making her visual assessment, carefully inspecting Nadia's furniture, trinkets, photos, and wall hangings. "You have a great eye for decorating," she complimented. "Smells good in here too."

"Thank you. I hope you two are hungry. I've got some great chicken and ribs for you."

"What kinda ribs? Are they pork?"

"Uh . . ." Actually Nadia had no clue; she hadn't clarified with Red, Hot, and Blue, and could only make an assumption. "Yes, ma'am," she guessed.

"Oh Lawd, I don't eat no pork."

Nadia's face flushed with embarrassment.

"That stuff will kill you, baby."

"Yes, ma'am." Her eyes darted over to Jonathan, who simply shrugged. "I don't really eat pork either," she lied, hoping Lola wouldn't find a reason to look into her deep freezer where there were packages of pork chops just waiting to be fried. "I just thought you two would enjoy it. There is still chicken, though." Nadia moved the dish of ribs off the table and set them on the kitchen counter.

"You may as well put that in the trash," Lola stated. "Give it here; I'll take care of it."

"No, ma'am." Nadia pulled back respectfully.

"You're a guest in my home and I can't have you doing that. It will be my pleasure to serve you tonight," she thought to say quickly before Lola could get her hands on the rib platter.

"That's sweet," Lola responded.

"If you'd like to go ahead and wash your hands before we eat, the bathroom is right down the hallway on the left."

"All right then."

Lola headed for the bathroom while Nadia eyed and whispered to Jonathan. "I should have asked what your mom doesn't eat."

"Don't worry about it. You had a backup ready."

"You gone wash your hands, Jonathan?" Lola asked in a way only a mother could.

"Yes, ma'am."

Nadia giggled at the obedient little boy in him. Minutes later they sat down for dinner with Lola saying the blessing over the meal.

"So, Jonathan tells me you work in manager developing or something like that."

"Yes, ma'am, I train leadership development to new management employees."

"Mmm-hmm," Lola commented, biting down into her chicken. "This is good, baby."

Jonathan winked at Nadia.

"Thank you," she responded, standing to her feet to get the phone. "Excuse me. I usually don't eat after a certain hour, so whoever this is calling doesn't realize it's dinnertime. It's probably my dad."

"What do you think, ma," Jonathan asked under his breath as Nadia turned her back to grab the phone in her kitchen.

"Pork? Mm, mm, mmph."

"Hello," Nadia answered. "This is she. . . . No, ma'am, I keep telling you all that I don't have an account there and I have dinner guests so I'm going to hang up now." Nadia hung on the phone a few more seconds, which gave Lola an opportunity to comment on what she'd heard.

"You betta check her credit."

"I'm sorry about that," Nadia apologized, taking her seat again, frustration apparent on her face. The phone calls were coming more and more frequently and had become unbearable. Nadia had started collecting information from each caller, making sure to get the company name, and whatever other information the collection agent would share. Most of the time, once Nadia made it clear that she wouldn't be making a payment of any amount, the agent would be far less than cooperative about sharing any account information. She had coaxed a few of the companies to send her statements, which nearly made her pass out in shock at the exorbitant balances and delinquent amounts. "I keep getting wrong number calls," Nadia tried to explain, slightly embarrassed.

"It's all right, baby," Lola commented.

"Are you enjoying your meal?" Nadia said, pasting on a hospitable smile.

"I am; thank you so much for having us over."

"My pleasure."

"So, what you think about that great big dog Jonathan got?" Lola tested.

"I've come to appreciate him a little more than I used to," Nadia admitted. Which was partially true. He had come in right handy that day Feenie came barging in the house.

"Jonathan told me you looked after him while he was away."

"Yes, ma'am. I did my best."

"You know, they say you can tell a lot about how people will treat a child by the way they treat a pet."

Nadia gulped, remembering the evenings she really didn't walk Pazzo at all but just took him down the street a bit until he went up under some bush. And the one time she'd forgotten to put out fresh food and water for him. "That's a very interesting observation, although I've never heard of it before. You didn't find any marks or bruises on Pazzo, did you?" she joked, looking at Jonathan.

"No, but I meant to ask you, did he have an accident in the house?" he asked with a crinkled brow.

"No." She gulped a second time, thinking about what Terryn had suggested about the presence of hidden cameras. "Not that I know of. Why? What's wrong?"

"I've just noticed him sniffing at the floor in my bedroom like he's marked it or something."

Nadia raised her eyebrows, shrugged, and shook her head slightly, while stuffing a hush puppy in her mouth. Covering her full mouth with a napkin, she mumbled, "Let me turn on a little music." While she was up, her phone rang once more. Again it was a debt collector looking for payment on an account that Nadia knew nothing of. This time Nadia took the time to gather as much information as she could from the call.

"I think you better leave this one alone, Jonathan," Lola warned.

CHAPTER 16

Rance examined the envelope that the card came in very carefully. It was stamped with an out-of-state postmark and had no return address and was mailed to his work office. The words glued inside the card made his blood boil. He was too angry to take the card seriously but too scared to ignore it and it was the second one he'd received.

Your September 3rd payment is now past due. This is your second and final warning. Deposit $4,000 into account number X5554321 by September 17 and $2,000 dollars each week thereafter.

Enclosed with the card was a picture of Laiken out in the front yard playing with the boys in the lawn sprinkler system.

After dialing Feenie's number, he nearly blew up once she answered her cell phone. "What is the meaning of this!" he bellowed.

"What are you hollering at me about, Rance?"

"How dare you demand more money out of

me, Feenie! I am paying you extremely well to take care of those girls, and just because you can't do your part, this is what you do? I wish I'd never laid eyes on you!"

"Well, you ought to be wishing that you'd kept your pants up, because I'm the least of your worries right now. I'm nothing compared to what your wife would take you to the cleaners for if she knew about these girls. And I'll tell you another thing— you can call Social Services or Child Protective Services if you want to! And if you think I'ma cover for your behind when they ask who their daddy is, you gone be in for the shock of your life, 'cause I know your name, your address, *and* your Social Security number. And if I go down, you best believe you going down right with me. So before you call here again you better think about all of that!" she screamed before snapping her phone closed.

She was glad that the girls were out of hearing range. She had taken them to the beach and they were having the time of their lives splashing around in the water. Feenie dropped her phone into her beach bag, then lay back on her towel thinking over what Rance had said to her. She hadn't asked him for any more money, not that she didn't think he should give her more. Quickly she sat up and dialed his number. As soon as he answered, she laid into him a second time. "And furthermore, ain't nobody asked you for no more money! I don't know what you're talking about."

"Then what about this letter, this card, Feenie? Don't try to play dumb. This little 'I know a secret' shenanigan."

"That must be one of your other baby mamas,"

she answered flatly. "But it ain't me, and even if I did ask for more money, you know you better come up off that dollar and the first time you don't your wife is gonna hear from me. And you *know* that's a fact."

Feenie snapped her phone closed a second time before Rance could utter another word.

This time it was him that sat pensively brooding over their conversation from the driver's seat of his car. The more he thought on it, the more he concluded that the culprit couldn't have been Feenie. She'd never sent a request for an increase this way and under this guise. This was completely out of the norm for her.

There were only a few other people in his circle who knew of Cara's and Mia's existence: his secretary, Cathy, who had kept so many of his indiscretions to herself, he highly doubted it was her; Sid, his tax accountant, who needed to know where this extra money was going to every month and for what purpose. He couldn't imagine that Sid would do something like this out of the clear blue sky. That left only one other person, Terryn Campbell.

Rance scrolled through the contact list on his phone until he found the number of a longtime colleague and friend. Pete Debusk.

"Pete, it's Rance."

"Well, hello, counselor," Pete answered jovially. "What can I do you for?"

"Listen, I got a situation that I need your help with. It's personal this time. How soon can you meet with me?"

"I can squeeze you in by the end of the week; how urgent is it?"

"Honestly I was hoping you had some free time this evening."

"You buying?"

"Whatever it takes," Rance answered desperately. "Just name the place."

"How about In Dulj at the Renaissance, say around six?"

"I'll be there."

Rance arrived at the hotel's lounge a half hour early with the two cards and photos, and got a head start on a cocktail. Right on time, Pete waltzed up to his table with an extended hand and took a seat after the two men shook.

"What's getting your goat, man? You sounded pretty frazzled on the phone." Pete, dressed in faded jeans and a white wrinkled oxford with rolled sleeves, a pair of worn-out Bass loafers, and a five o'clock shadow, flagged the waitress over and rattled off his drink order.

"I know this goes without saying, but this is completely confidential."

"Rance, you're talking to a PI."

"I know. Just feels better to say it anyway." Rance reached into his messenger bag, pulled out a legal-sized envelope, and slid it across the table. "I need to know who's doing this to me." He lifted his drink from the table and gulped it down, while Pete emptied the envelope's contents on the table, then reviewed them. Pete studied the picture of the two girls for a few seconds, then the photo of Feenie.

"Man, please tell me this isn't what it looks like."

Rance simply nodded, unable to meet Pete

eye-to-eye. He shot his eyes around the lounge, looking for their waitress as a distraction.

"And Laiken has no idea," Pete said more as a statement than a question.

"Not a clue." This time Rance did look squarely at Pete.

Pete pushed a puff of air through his lips. "Any idea who it might be?"

"Yeah. I just fired a paralegal about six weeks back." Rance nodded slowly. "I think she's seeking revenge."

"What's her name?" Pete asked, taking a scrap of paper out of his shirt pocket.

"Terryn Campbell."

"Got an address?"

"Yeah." Rance dug through his bag again for Terryn's address, which he'd had Cathy pull from her employee file. He'd also found a photo from an office staff party, which he slid over to Pete.

"So, what's the backstory?" Pete thanked the waitress for his drink, then turned his attention back to Rance, who filled him in on how he'd come about having a set of twins that his wife knew nothing about, and how he'd been able to keep it away from his wife. Pete nearly spewed his drink across the table when Rance quoted to him what he'd been paying Feenie in hush money. "You sure it's not her trying to get more?"

"I'm pretty positive it's not her. This is not her modus operandi," he answered, shaking his head with a sigh.

"Who else knows about these girls?"

"No one else that would do this besides the woman I fired."

"All right, well, I got enough to get started at least. I'll let you know what I find."

"Thanks, Pete."

"I'll send you my bill."

"I wouldn't have it any other way."

"In the meantime, you might want to go ahead and make a deposit into this account—buy you some time."

Rance groaned but knew it would be better to take Pete's advice than to have Laiken find out before he could put a stop to this ploy.

The men shook and made small talk over a few more drinks before going separate ways. Rance drove home to his wife and boys, and Pete, using the address Rance had given him, headed over to the Crescent at Fells Point to begin finding information on Terryn.

That following Friday, Terryn drove to the library, signed in to use the computer as usual, and logged in to the Washington Mutual checking account she'd established. She smiled to herself when she saw that Rance had responded to her mailings, and a four-thousand-dollar deposit had been made. After deleting the computer's history tracking, then visiting twelve more random sites, she headed to the nearest ATM to put some cash in her pocket. Taking out as much as the ATM would allow, Terryn decided to treat herself to a manicure and pedicure, and a few new dresses. She later swung by the mall and made the minimum payments on her credit card accounts, then stopped at the grocery store to pick up a rotisserie chicken, a bag of salad mix, a tomato, cucumbers, Caesar dressing, and wraps.

All the way home, she blasted Mary J. Blige's "Just Fine" from her car stereo, singing and meaning its words. "I won't change my life, my life's just fine, fine, fine, fine, fine, fine wooo!" She popped her fingers and swung her head until she pulled onto Bernsdale Drive and noticed police cars in front of Feenie's house.

One hour earlier

"Nine-one-one, please state your emergency." The operator's voice came across the phone line into Cara's ear. With a mouthful of giggles she hung up.

"Let me do it," Mia begged, taking the phone from her twin. She pressed in the digits and waited for the operator's response.

"Nine-one-one, please state your emergency." As Cara had done before her, Mia immediately hung up the phone and giggled. Seconds later, the phone rang back. Both girls inspected the caller ID, and when they didn't identify the number of the city's emergency response team calling back, they allowed the phone to ring. After three attempts, the phone finally silenced and the girls lost interest, going into the living room to watch cartoons. Within five minutes there was a solid knock at the door that startled both girls.

"Shh! Don't say anything," Cara ordered. Holding each other's hands, they sat motionless on the couch staring blankly at the television. They jumped again at the second knock.

"Police, open up," a male voice charged. Right away Mia began to cry.

"Be quiet!" Cara snapped, snatching her sister by the arm, which only made Mia wail louder.

Once more the policeman rapped loud and hard, ordering for the door to be opened. From the call he'd gotten from the 911 operator, and by the crying he suddenly heard, he discerned that there was a child home alone. Quickly he changed his tone and coaxed Cara to open the door. "I need you to open the door, sweetie, it's the police."

Though terrified, Cara stood her ground for as long as she could. "My mama said not to open the door for anybody."

"If you don't open the door, I'm going to have to kick it down." He gave Cara a few seconds to think about it, then asked her a final time to open. Not knowing what else to do, Cara twisted the dead bolt lock to the right, turned the knob, and slowly opened the front door of their home, while Mia sat on the couch sniveling. "Who's here with you, sweetie?" Officer Thomas asked gently.

"Just my sister, right there." Cara stood back a bit and pointed to the couch.

"Where's your mommy and daddy?" a second, female officer asked, while Officer Thomas began doing a quick search of the home, looking in closets and behind other closed doors.

"My mommy went to get a Brazilian wax, and my daddy doesn't live here," she answered.

"What's your mommy's name?"

"Jerrafine Trotter."

"And what's your daddy's name?"

"Rance Alexander."

"That's your sister right there?"

"Yes. Her name is Mia and my name is Cara. We're twins," she volunteered. "You guys scared her when you knocked on the door so hard."

"Well, we didn't mean to scare you, sweetie, but we were worried about you. You girls called 911 but you didn't say anything. We thought something had happened to you. How old are you girls?"

"We seven. Our birthday is on the Fourth of July."

"Really? That is so special," the officer said with a smile.

Officer Thomas came down after doing an upstairs search. "There's no one here," he said lowly while shaking his head. "How long has your mommy been gone?" he asked, looking at each of the girls. Mia still sat paralyzed on the couch, while Cara answered all the questions.

"I don't know exactly, but it was, like, when *Sesame Street* come on."

"Do you girls have food here?"

"Yes."

"Do you have bread and milk and cereal?" he asked, trying to determine if the children had been abandoned.

"Yes."

"How about orange juice?"

"I don't think so, but we have some Capri Suns if you would like one," she offered innocently.

"No, thank you," he chuckled. "Do you girls know what time your mommy will be back?"

"No, she just said she will be back after a while."

"We're going to have to call CPS," Officer Thomas stated to his partner. "Okay, you girls just sit there and finish watching cartoons. We're going to be right outside, but we won't leave you girls alone, okay?"

"Okay."

The two officers went out to their patrol cars and contacted Child Protective Services to take the twins into custody. After making the call, they waited around casually for someone from CPS to arrive.

"You always crying," Cara reprimanded her sister. "If you would have just shut up we could have acted like no one was home and they would have gone away!"

"Well, you started it by calling 911 in the first place," Mia shot back in her defense. "You always doing stuff to get us in trouble."

"You was calling them too," Cara retorted.

"So, you started it. I told you we didn't need to be calling nobody, but you went in there to call Daddy when you know Mommy told us not to do that. Now we might have to go to jail!"

"No, we don't, stupid."

"Yes, we do, for playing on the phone," Mia wailed. "You always doing something!"

"Just shut up!"

The girls argued back and forth for close to thirty minutes before the door swung open again with a frantic Feenie followed by the two officers, who'd already confirmed her identity when she pulled up in her vehicle and jumped out of her truck at the sight of police cars in her driveway. Every neighbor had found some reason to be outside near her house. She wanted to cuss them all out and tell them where to go, but she thought better of it in the officers' presence.

"Ma'am, your girls were here dialing 911 and hanging up. When the operators called back, there was no answer, which prompted our visit to your home today."

"Well, I had just run out for a minute to take care of something," Feenie tried to explain, panicked.

"At seven years old, these girls are just too young to be left alone by themselves."

"Yes, sir," Feenie acknowledged humbly.

"I'm going to have to write you a summons for child neglect," he announced.

Feenie gasped dramatically. "Sir, I just did it this one time, to take care of something important," she lied. "I assure you it won't happen again; can you just give me a warning or something?"

"No, ma'am, I can't do that."

"Please, sir, I promise it won't happen again," she said a second time, her eyes welling with tears.

"I'm sorry. Can I see your ID please?"

With shaking hands, Feenie dug her driver's license out of her wallet and handed it to Officer Thomas.

"And also, I have to let you know that CPS has been called, so they will be contacting you in a few days."

Feenie was too stunned to comment.

"We'll be right back." The female officer turned to the girls. "Girls, you did the right thing by calling 911, okay? You did nothing wrong. Just next time be sure to say something, okay?"

"Okay," they answered in unison.

Feenie was ready to blow up at her daughters but knew she couldn't if she planned to stay out of jail. She was so angry she couldn't even stand the sight of them. Nonetheless, she held her peace and took a seat in her living room waiting for Officer Thomas to hand her the summons. Ten minutes later, he returned with a sheet for her to sign and explained to her when her court date was.

"Do you have any questions for us?"

"No, sir," she said, keeping her humble front.

"All right. Good-bye, girls."

"Bye." They waved.

Feenie closed the door, then lit right into her children. "Why were y'all in here calling 911!"

"We didn't call them, Mommy."

"Yes, you did!" she screamed. Neither girl spoke a single word until she asked again, "What were y'all doing to be in here calling 911 playing on the phone!" Again the girls denied it, which made Feenie's blood boil. She held her hands together to keep from slapping both of them in their little lying mouths, but only because she knew CPS would be asking all kinds of questions and she dared not risk putting her hands or any bruises on them. She was itching to go break a switch off a tree and give them a lickin' like they had never had before, but again, felt the risk and consequence would be too high. "Y'all had to call them, or else the police would not have been here. And I want to know why you did that."

The girls would not bend on their stories that they had not called.

"The phone kept ringing and we didn't know who it was so we just didn't answer it," Mia stated.

"And we didn't call nobody," Cara added.

"You know what, y'all two just need to get outta my face before I seriously hurt you!" Feenie screamed, causing the girls to scurry up the steps. "Now I might have to go to jail just because y'all wanted to be in here playing on the phone! Then who y'all gone stay with? And I got news for you, your raggedy daddy ain't tryna have y'all up in his house!"

Angry at the world, Feenie collapsed on the couch. She was angry with the girls for playing on the phone, angry at Rance for getting her pregnant in the first place, and then angrier still that he'd left her with the girls to raise alone. She was angry with herself for not taking the girls with her to the spa, but there was just no room for them there. She was angry with her family for living too far away to keep the girls. She was just angry. She sat with a scowl on her face for a full two hours just wanting to choke someone.

"Mommy, can we please have something to eat now?" Mia had tiptoed down the stairs after working up the nerve.

"I will call you when I get ready to feed you!" Feenie barked, tempted out of her anger to send the twins to bed hungry. Instead she made them wait another thirty minutes before she got up to prepare a meal, which was simply beans and franks. She slammed the two plates on the table, then went to her bedroom before she instructed the girls to go eat, not wanting to see their faces. "And you better not go to bed with that kitchen dirty!"

CHAPTER 17

"Daddy, I promise you, I didn't open up these accounts and I don't have a clue why they are in my name," Nadia said in tears viewing her online credit report. "There's all kinds of stuff up here."

"E-mail me a copy of it so I can take a look at it. I'll be up there this weekend."

Nadia copied and pasted her information and sent it over to Aidan. "Somebody has stolen my identity, Daddy."

"Yeah, that's what it sounds like."

Together on the phone, they went through all the items listed. The accounts that actually belonged to Nadia were all current and reflected no late payments, but the ones she knew nothing about were seriously delinquent and over the credit limits. There was twenty-seven thousand dollars of delinquent debt in her name, and her credit score was completely trashed.

"We're going to have to get an attorney on this," Aidan advised. "Go ahead and start searching for one, and when I get there we can go pay him a visit together."

"Okay, I will," Nadia promised before ending the call. Just as she hung up the phone, Terryn came in with shopping bags.

"Girl, what did you do, hit the lottery or something?" Nadia gawked.

"No, my brother sent me a few dollars to help me get by until something comes through. I have a little something for you too for letting me stay here."

"Well, you know you don't have to do that right now, but I do accept all donations!" Nadia giggled through her tears. "And why did I find out that, just like you said, somebody did steal my identity and has run up a ton of debt in my name?"

"Oh no! Is there anything you can do about it?"

"Well, I have to file a police report, and mail it to all the creditors to have the accounts closed, and you know when I talked to them, they all harassed me for all types of money. I'm going to have to retain a lawyer or something to help me work through all of it. I'm just glad I'm finding out about it before they started garnishing my paycheck!"

"That is so terrible! But I bet I have something that will make you feel a little better." Terryn started reaching in her bag.

"A McDonald's cheeseburger would cheer me up right now!" Nadia smirked, trying to ease the pain of her credit findings.

"I wish you would have told me that before I bought you this." Terryn pulled out a pair of Pammie striped rubber boots from Coach, and Nadia screamed.

"I will take those over a cheeseburger any day!"

"I thought you would. It was the least I could do for you letting me stay here," Terryn added with a smile.

"Thank you so much, Terryn!" Nadia slipped her feet into the boots although she still had on her Nine West Techno Twill suit from work, which really did no justice to the boots. She stood and pranced around the living room while Terryn sang the lyrics to Mariah Carey's "Touch My Body."

"Oh-ay-oh, oh-ay-oh," they sang together, then sat on the couch, where Nadia had her laptop open.

"So, what's good with you and Jonathan?" Terryn asked. "How was dinner the other night? You work so much, we haven't even had a chance to talk about it."

"I don't know. He's been kind of distant since he and his mom was here. I think she's mad at me 'cause I had pork ribs." Terryn burst into laughter. "No joke! When she found out the ribs were pork she was all like, 'that will kill you' and tried to take them out of my hand and throw them in the trash!"

"No, she didn't."

"You know I wasn't be throwing my money away! I was like, 'naw, Mama Lola. Go'n somewhere and sit down now.'" Nadia waved her hand as if she were shooing away flies. "She is supposed to be cooking this weekend and I'm supposed to go over there. Maybe my daddy can come with me. That would be funny, him and his mom, me and my dad . . . hmm. Anyway," she continued, "how's your job search coming?"

"I got a couple of things lined up for next week," Terryn said, tossing a few strands of hair out of her face.

"Cool. Where at?" Nadia asked for general purposes.

"A couple of offices downtown."

"Well, I hope you get the one you really want."

"Me too, or else my brother's going to have to send me some more dough, you know?" she chuckled, rubbing her thumb against her fingers. "He did agree to help me get a new place, so I'll probably be gone in about two more weeks."

That was great news to Nadia, not that Terryn was a bad roommate, but hey, the sooner the better, she thought.

"You know I know about that, as much money as my dad has had to give me."

Terryn cringed inside at the thought. Nadia's phone rang, bringing a look of dread to her face. Every time it rang now, it was someone asking her for money that she honestly did not owe.

"You want me to get that?" Terryn asked, rising to her feet and gathering her wares.

"Nope, let it ring," Nadia huffed, turning back to her laptop. "Let me get back to figuring this mess out."

"Well, call me if you need me to do anything. Anything besides wash the dishes, that is." A few seconds later Terryn's bedroom door closed, signifying that she was probably in for the night.

As much as Nadia tried to focus on her now shady credit, her mind kept going back to dinner the other night with Jonathan and his mom, especially knowing he was such a mama's boy and that she had to approve of his relationships. She hated that she thought about him so much, though. What really did it for her was that day he took her out to the park. Initially Nadia was madder than a cluster of disturbed wasps, but as dusk began to set in, Jonathan pointed straight ahead of them, which was where the sun was beginning to set.

"I know you were probably wondering why I brought you here," he'd said. "But look there; isn't it beautiful?" And it truly was, Nadia had to admit. He turned from facing the table directly to straddling the bench right behind her and wrapped his arms around her chest and shoulders, inviting Nadia to lean back into him. And for the next ten minutes or so, they sat silent, with him planting a tiny kiss behind her ear every few seconds.

He felt good. Real good.

Nadia wanted to ask him some questions about the two of them, but words would have really messed up the moment, so she kept silent. Plus, she already knew that she would have to pass the Lola Strickland test first. And really, Nadia didn't see how she could have scored poorly. In minutes she'd forgotten all about her credit and thought solely of Jonathan's mother's potential assessment.

My house was immaculately clean . . . well, except for the few boxes that Terryn had scooted right behind the couch from her move in. And Ms. Lola did compliment me on my decorating skills. The dinner went pretty well minus the ribs, so she probably thinks I can cook pretty well. And I was respectful enough and answered all her questions, and was dressed appropriately for dinner in my home. Well, maybe I should have worn a whole shirt instead of a sleeveless blouse, but I didn't see her look at me any kind of way. I'm sure I did just fine.

And let me not forget about Jonathan's little shortcomings either. Well, his paycheck is superb; that's a huge plus, but those Prozac, I mean bipolar pills is something for me to think about. But wait a minute . . . I didn't actually see the medicine. But neither did I look in all the places that medicine could be. Like in his luggage! He was away on a business trip, and if he is on bipolar meds, he would need to take those with him! Duh! Okay. I can't be dealing with no man who might flip on me in the snap of a finger.

Now, the size-large condoms are a plus. If he really needs a size large. That could all be a part of his ego. Maybe he just thinks he needs a large. Do condoms come in size small? I will have to make it a point to look the next time I go to the drugstore. And suppose he's really not a large, and he's really a regular using a large. That would be a mess. But I have to give him points for using condoms in the first place. But who is he using them with? If it's Feenie, oh my goodness, that's going to be it for me. I don't want nothing that woman has had. Nothing!

And if it is Feenie, then again comes the point that Jonathan might be a minute man. But then again, maybe not. Maybe he is a minute man if he only got a few minutes, or really not that interested and so only wants to take a few minutes. Because there is nothing worse than taking all day with somebody who you'd just rather hurry up and get it over with with. I learned that from college. I got so tired of my then-boyfriend trying to act like he had some mad sex skills taking all night to do a little bit of nothing. Faking only works for about seven minutes; then you just have to shut up and only speak when spoken to. Oh yeah—back to Jonathan. Anyway, he probably is really not a minute man, he just has to be interested. And I think he's interested in me. I can tell from the way he held me when we were watching that sunset that night.

Okay, now this dog thing. That is a tough one. I have to say, I've grown a bit when it comes to Pazzo. But I don't love him or nothing. I still think he's nasty. And what about what his mama said about the way a person treats pets? What was that about? First of all, if I had a kid I would never have him on a leash galloping him or her up and down the street. And I would never think of making them eat out of a bowl on the floor. I mean, unless we were pretending to be puppies or something. Kids like that kind of stuff. And I certainly wouldn't make them sleep outside in a little nasty dark hut. I don't think his mama knows what she is talking about when it comes to that. If me and Jonathan had a kid, that child would be so spoiled! Pet schmet!

Even so, I don't think the dog thing is worse than the mama's boy thing. But then again, I don't know how bad it is. Maybe he's just a little bit of a mama's boy. No. Not if he lets her chose his girlfriends. He got it bad. I don't think I want to deal with all that.

"She's a nice girl, but I don't know about her just yet," Lola started, crossing her feet at the ankles and leaning back in a leather recliner purchased especially for her visits.

"What don't you know about her, Ma?"

"Well, for one she eats pork. If she eats it, she'll feed it to you and I can't have her tryna kill you off."

"I don't think she was trying to kill anyone. You heard her say that she only cooked it because she thought you would enjoy it."

"Yeah, her cooking. That's another thing. How she gonna try to pass them people's cooking off as her own?"

"What people?" Jonathan took a seat on his couch, patted it twice for Pazzo to join him, and rubbed his head when he did.

"She ain't cook that food. You ain't see that big ol' Red, Hot, and Blue bag sitting in the kitchen? Probably had them hush puppies in it. If she wansn't gonna cook, that's all she had to say, but don't sit up there and act like you cooked it when you didn't. Ain't nothing wrong with saying, oh, I ordered in. That's why people have catering menus. You better find out if that girl can cook for real."

"Yes, ma'am."

"'Cause even with as much money as you make, when you get married you ain't gonna want to eat out all the time. Eatin' out sometimes is nice, but not all the time. Sometimes you gonna want a home-cooked meal and I'm not gonna be here to cook it for you. Not unless you gonna give me some kind of mother-in-law suite. Well, really a mother suite, 'cause I ain't your in-law."

Jonathan held his breath, hoping that she wouldn't press that issue. He loved Lola but didn't want her around like that.

"She looks like she knows how to keep a house, though. Unless she got Molly Maid to come in there today."

"And what if she did? What's wrong with that?"

"Nothing's wrong with it, but can she keep the house herself? What's gonna happen if y'all can't afford the maid people? Then what? Is she going to be able to keep the place clean? 'Cause you ain't gonna want to come home to no dirty house either."

"You right about that," Jonathan agreed.

"And it's good that you let her keep the dog. She do all right with him?"

"Yeah, he looked fine when I got back. Well taken care of."

"Good. That's a good sign. Now, who was that ringing on her phone? 'Cause that sounded like some bill collector calls to me."

"I don't know, Ma, I wasn't the one answering her phone."

"You better make sure you check her credit."

CHAPTER 18

Feenie had called Rance first thing in the morning crying and scared of the consequences she now faced after leaving the twins home alone. Her words came across the phone line in anger and disgust more than a plea for help as she'd intended.

"You need to come get these hardheaded, ungrateful girls!"

"What's going on, Jerrafine?"

"Their little fast behinds 'bout to have me in jail!" she screamed. "And you need to come get them *today*! They done messed around and got me up on some charges." Through shouts and screams, Feenie explained to Rance what had taken place, claiming that she'd only gone to a neighbor's house for a few minutes to help rearrange some furniture. "It took a little longer than we thought it would, and when I got back, they got the police standing all in my front yard!"

"Feenie, the girls have told me that you leave them quite frequently," Rance stated calmly. "And I've seen you do it myself."

"All I am saying is, you better come get these

little high-yellow no-neck monsters before I hurt them!"

Quickly Rance jotted down Feenie's words on a notepad.

"Now I gotta go through a CPS investigation and go to court in two weeks. But I guess that don't matter to you 'cause you got your little white picket fence life going on, huh?"

"Feenie, if you need lawyer representation, I can refer you to someone, but I can't represent you myself. There is a conflict of interest there."

"How? How, Rance? You ain't interested in taking these girls, so how is it a conflict of interest? Seems to me you'd do a mighty fine job convincing the judge of why the girls should stay with me and why I would be the best parent to keep them so your nose and hands can stay clean," she snapped.

"Jerrafine, I will be happy to refer you to another attorney if you'd like."

"No, what I'd like is for you to come get your damn kids!" At that Feenie slammed the phone down.

Rance sighed as he thought for the one thousandth time of the mess he'd gotten himself into. Every day it was becoming more and more clear what he needed to do. In addition to paying Feenie, Rance had painfully paid out an additional ten thousand dollars to keep his daughters' existence from his wife, and just wasn't willing to do it anymore. It was time to come clean.

He called Laiken at eleven and told her to expect him home around two. "We need to talk," he'd stated, reasoning that this would be the best time to tell her since his boys were away at his parents' home in Florida for two weeks. They'd been gone for three days and Laiken had tried to turn on a little spice while they were away, only to get a less than welcoming response from her husband. It had been at least two years since they'd been free of the boys, but instead of playing chase around the house, Rance was too heavily laden to enjoy his wife. Preparing himself for the worst, he slid his key into the lock of his front door, and opened it as if it were the entrance to a tomb of curses.

"Laiken," he called from the front door. "Laiken, where are you?" He loosened his tie from his neck as he set his bag down in the foyer. When he looked up, his wife stood before him clad in one of his shirts with the buttons undone and a tiny white thong.

"Thought you'd never get here," she said sexily. "I've been waiting all day to get my hands on you." She slinked up to Rance and let her hands do the talking while she leaned in for a kiss. Surprisingly, Rance only pecked her lips and pushed her hands away.

"Sweetie, we need to talk." He led her to the couch and almost forced her to sit down, while he stood and paced for a few seconds before taking a seat beside her. "Laiken." He found it hard to look his wife in the eye, so he stared at her hands instead as he took them into his own. "I don't even know where to start, but I've got to tell you this."

"What. What is it?" she asked, her settling fear apparent in her voice.

"I . . . I have not always done the right thing. I've not always made the right decisions, and because of that, I . . . what I am about to tell you is just . . ." He swallowed as he focused on a vase on the table. "Laiken, I have two daughters by another woman."

"Wha . . . ? You what?"

Rance shook his head and blew out a long breath. "I was so stupid. I slept with this woman some years back and . . . ." Before he could finish his sentence Laiken had stood and tried her best to slap the taste out of his mouth. Rance didn't retaliate, but took the blow he knew was sure to come.

"You lying, dirty, cheating, filthy . . . !" Laiken searched her mind for other words, but none of them justly described how she viewed the man sitting in front of her. "You have other kids?" she repeated incredulously, followed by a flurry of curse words and several wild slaps to Rance's head. He only put forth his hands to restrain her, knowing she had every right to be infuriated. "How old are these little bastards of yours!" she spat once Rance calmed her down a bit.

"Seven-year-old twins," he answered shamefully.

"Seven! You've been sneaking around here lying to my face while I've been playing the good wife to you for seven years!" Laiken smeared her tears and makeup away with the palm of her hands. "Here I am, washing your clothes, and raising your two rambunctious boys, cooking your meals, picking up your dry cleaning, and keeping this house spotless for you to enjoy when you come home, and you don't think any more of me than to go out here and screw some whore in the streets?" Her eyes narrowed to slits as she paused, but not expecting Rance to reply. "Who is she, Rance?" When he didn't answer soon enough, she swung at his head again. "You tell me who this wench is right now!" she demanded.

"Her name is Jerrafine Trotter. She's a former client of mine." Rance paused momentarily to finally look in his wife's eyes. "Laiken, I am so sorry."

"Don't you sit here and apologize, Rance Michael Alexander. You've fathered some woman's kids and have kept it hidden for seven years! You know what, sorry is right! You *are* sorry!" she screamed at the top of her lungs.

"I deserve every bit of this, Laiken, and you don't. The boys don't. But I couldn't keep it from you any longer," he said remorsefully.

"And why is that, because you've decided to run off and be with your other family? Is that it? Are you leaving us, Rance!" she sneered.

"No. I—"

"Yes, you are! You are leaving! You are getting your stuff and"—Laiken leapt to her feet, charged toward the front door, picking up Rance's laptop bag on the way, yanked the door open and threw the bag onto the front lawn—"getting out of here."

"Laiken, calm down."

"Don't you dare tell me to calm down! You come stumbling in here every night like you've slaved away at work all day in your office and in court and come to find out you've been playing house with another family! Get out! Get out now!" When Rance didn't move, Laiken's adrenaline drove her to try to push him from the couch, but her 120-pound frame did nothing against Rance's frame, a full hundred pounds heavier than hers.

"I'll leave but not until we finish talking about it."

"What else is there to say, Rance? Huh? What else is there? What is she, blackmailing you or something? She wants to come live here? She wants her girls to finally meet their brothers?" she said, emphasizing the word *brothers* with fingered quotation marks.

"No. I want them to meet their brothers," Rance stated, not ready to tell his wife that he was being blackmailed, but felt he needed an avenue to ease the girls in just in case Feenie had to serve time. He couldn't have his daughters being awarded to the state of Maryland and in the foster care system. He loved them too much to let that happen despite the way he'd kept them at a distance.

"What! You want to bring those bastard girls over here and expect us to just accept them like we're the freaking Brady Bunch?"

"Please don't ask me to choose, Laiken. I've chosen you and the boys over them for far too long, and it's high time that I stand up and do what's right. And if that means I lose what we have, then—"

"What we have? What we have is a house built on a pack of lies! If that's what you want, you can have it!" she ended with a shout as she pulled her wedding ring off her finger and hurled it across the room before storming upstairs to their bedroom and slamming the door.

Rance sat silently and motionless for ten minutes, overwhelmed by his sea of thoughts, but at the same time feeling a strange sense of relief that the secret was finally out. The buzzing of his cell phone on his hip startled him. After reaching to get it, Rance answered in a rush when he saw Pete's number reflected on his caller ID. "Pete; hey, guy," he said, trying to cover his distress with an upbeat tone.

"Got some news for you. You free tonight?" Pete took a drag off a cigarette, dropped it to the floor, and extinguished it with his foot.

"Just name the place and I'm there."

"Same spot, same time."

Rance backed out of his driveway and switched on his stereo, which was tuned to an easy listening station. The Eagles were singing "Hotel California," but the music wasn't easy enough to calm Rance's thoughts or mind. He knew it could be no one but Terryn taking advantage of the information she had, but he planned to put a stop to that no sooner than Pete was able to confirm. When he arrived at the lounge, Pete sat munching on an order of hot wings and enjoying a beer.

"So, what do you have for me?" Rance asked anxiously.

"Have a seat, man. It's not what you think."

"Huh? Well then, who is it?"

Pete handed a plain manila folder over to Rance. "Take a look at that photo."

Rance studied the picture of a black female with

her hair pulled back in a ponytail, enjoying a cup
of coffee at Starbucks and reading a magazine.

"You know 'er?"

"Not at all. Who is this? I don't know this
woman." Pete raised his brows slightly in surprise.

"Maybe a former lover?"

"No," Rance denied right away. "I don't believe I've ever seen or met this woman before in
my life." Rance studied the picture a few seconds
longer. "What's her name?"

"Nadia Mitchell. That is who the bank account
is linked to. Set up at the library down on
Sulpher Spring Road about two months ago."

"Nadia, Nadia . . ." Rance chanted, trying to get
the name to ring a bell. With a perplexed look on
his face, he shook his head. "I don't know this
woman from a can of paint. Where does she live?"

"Twenty-seven thirteen Bernsdale."

"Bernsdale? That's the street Jerrafine lives on.
Must be a friend of hers whom she's obviously
coerced into some of her own money-laundering
schemes. What else do you know about her?"

"Works a full-time job, single, no dependents,
drives a Honda Accord. Looks like she has a
friend staying with her . . . a female."

Rance took the folder of information, gulped
down the remainder of his drink, thanked his
friend, then headed to his car. With a lead foot he
weaved in and out of traffic and turned corners
like a maniac to get to 2713 Bernsdale Drive.

In twenty minutes, he turned onto the street,
glanced at Feenie's house, noting that her truck
was in the driveway, then slowed down as he passed
the next few homes until he reached Nadia's.

Angry but composed, he lifted himself from the driver's seat, strode to the front door, and rang the bell. A few seconds later, Nadia pulled her door open.

"Yes?" she answered with raised brows. Rance was silent initially until Nadia spoke again. "Can I help you?"

"Why? What's your motive?" he asked, becoming angrier as he talked.

"Sir, I don't know what you're talking about."

"I'm talking about this!" Rance whipped the first card out of the folder he held in his hand and held it close to Nadia's face.

Quickly Nadia read the words. "I'm sorry, I do not know who you are and what this is about."

"You know what this is about!" Rance snarled, beginning to lose his patience.

"No. I really don't. I need you to leave my property before I call the police."

Rance stared at Nadia deliberately, his vision bouncing from one of her eyes to the other, looking for truth or lie.

"So you didn't send this?" he asked with skepticism, showing her the card again.

"I've never seen it before."

"Is your name Nadia Mitchell?"

"Yes, but, sir, I don't know you." Just then a bulb went off in Nadia's head. "Oh my goodness!" she gasped. "You know what, I just found out that my identity has been stolen and this probably has something to do with it! Can I see that information again?"

Not taking his eyes off her face, Rance opened the folder to show Nadia the two cards and a printout of banking information that displayed her name across the top. She let out a heavy sigh. "I don't know who has gotten a hold of my information, but they are ruining my life!"

"So you don't know anything about this?"

"No! I have about twenty-seven thousand dollars' worth of debt that I don't know anything about. I wish I knew more."

Rance closed the folder and tucked it under his arm. "Well, I'll tell you what. Do you mind taking my number and if you find out anything, can you give me a call and let me know, and I'll do the same for you?"

"Yes, that would help me so much," Nadia agreed. She accepted the card from his hands and her heart almost stopped when she read his name, suddenly realizing that he was Terryn's former boss. She couldn't help but gasp.

"What's wrong?"

Her eyes floated from his card to his face and back again. "I think I know who's doing this to you."

"Is that right?"

Nadia nodded slowly. "Come on in."

Rance obliged, entering and having a seat on Nadia's couch.

"Now, I don't know you personally, but we definitely know someone in common."

"And who is that, Jerrafine, down the street?"

"Yeah, I know her too, but she's not who I had in mind. My girlfriend used to work for you," Nadia stated. "But you fired her. At least that's what she told me."

"Terryn Campbell."

"Exactly. We were roommates in college, and she just got finished staying here for a few weeks. She moved out just a week ago," Nadia informed him. "It's all making sense now. Because after she got fired, she asked if she could stay here, saying that she didn't have the money to pay rent, but then about a week later, she comes in with all these packages, claiming that her brother had sent her money. If you don't mind me asking, did you start paying her?"

Rance nodded in shame. "Yeah, I did."

"You have twin girls who live down the street, right?"

"How'd you know?" Rance had purposely removed the photos of Feenie and the girls from the folder before confronting Nadia.

"I think it was me that was on the phone that day that you caught her sharing your personal information; then she called me later and told me she'd been fired."

Rance nodded, adding the story up.

"We've been friends for years, and she could easily have gotten my information to open a bank account," Nadia pondered. "I'm sure it's her. It has to be." She folded her arms across her chest and stared blankly toward her TV screen although it was off. "It has to be her."

"And you said someone has stolen your identity?"

"Yeah. I'm wondering if that could have been her too," she added, chewing on her bottom lip.

"Would you like me to take a look at it for you?" Rance offered, clearly seeing Nadia's sincerity and brewing anger for what she suspected Terryn had done.

"Oh, would I! If you don't mind, that would be great. Oh, but wait—right now I'm in so much debt, I wouldn't be able to pay you."

"You know what? I will do this one pro bono if I can get to the bottom of this," he promised as he stood to his feet.

"I'd like to get to the bottom of it myself."

"I appreciate your time, Ms. Mitchell." Rance extended his hand for a shake. "You said Terryn just moved into an apartment?"

"Yeah. I have the address around here somewhere." They released hands and Nadia walked over to her kitchen counter, where she had a stack of mail and a few random notes. "Here it is." She copied the information down on a sticky note and handed it to Rance.

"Thank you. Thanks for your time and your help."

"No, thank you. I think we both learned something tonight."

"And if you talk to Ms. Campbell, I would advise you not to let on to anything."

"Okay," Nadia agreed." As soon as Rance left, she called her dad.

Terryn sighed as she dropped her last box of belongings onto her living room floor and looked around her new apartment with a smile. Getting money out of Rance was like taking candy from a baby. She turned on her stereo to get her excited about getting settled, and began unpacking the boxes she'd pulled out of storage over the past few days.

By the time six hours had passed, Terryn had the place looking as if she'd been there two years. With everything neat and in its place, she took a seat on her living room sofa with a tall glass of water, and logged on to her laptop. It was payday, and Rance always paid on time, but just in case he decided to show out, Terryn faithfully checked her account every Friday afternoon.

With light nimble fingers, she keyed in her user name and password, clicked on Account Information, then tightened her lips into a ball. Her deposit for the week had not been made.

"Oh, this man thinks I'm playing with him!" Wasting no time, Terryn dug through an unpacked box and retrieved her blackmailing supplies. Before the sun went down, she'd cut and pasted her final warning, then drove into D.C. to mail it. She didn't have time to send it out of state to her brother to ask him to drop it in the mail for her, but she didn't want to risk it being mailed too close to the city.

Bethany Miller decided to meet the girls at the playground rather than coming out to Feenie's home, knowing she could get the girls to talk more openly if they felt free to laugh and play. She would do a home visit later as part of her routine investigation. She'd asked Feenie to stay seated on a nearby bench, but clearly in the girls' sight while she talked to them. Feenie was scared to cooperate, but even more afraid of what not cooperating might mean, so dressed in jeans and an elongated baby-blue T-shirt, Feenie took a seat and prayed that the girls wouldn't say too much. She watched as they and Bethany headed for the swings. They each took a seat, with Bethany between them, kicked their feet out, and propelled themselves toward the sky for a few minutes in laughter. Then they skipped to the seesaws, where the girls got on while Bethany stood in the middle. Next they headed to a dome-shape jungle gym, leaned against the bars and began to talk. Feenie's hands began to sweat although it was only seventy degrees outside. Every now and then, one of the girls would flip around a bar, or begin to climb upward, only to jump down again and return to Bethany's side. After about twenty minutes, Bethany made her way back over to Feenie.

"Ms. Trotter, the girls had an awful lot to say, and I will be frank with you; I'm very concerned." Feenie was too afraid to comment. "From what they shared, we're going to have to do a full investigation of your interaction with and caregiving of your children."

"I mean, is that really necessary? You can see we live in a nice clean home and they are clean and well cared for."

"That doesn't exactly mean that your home is safe, or that they are in a nurturing environment. And to be honest with you, some of what they had to say would cause me to believe that there are some areas where safety and nurturing may be lacking."

"So, what are you trying to say? I don't know

how to raise my kids?" Feenie snapped, beginning to take offense.

"No, I'm not saying that at all. I am saying that the girls revealed some things that are cause for alarm."

"Like what? I treat them girls good!"

"Well, I can tell you that they shared that you frequently leave them home alone while you run errands and go out for the evening."

"They are lying!" Feenie jumped to her feet. "Cara, Mia! Y'all get over here!"

"Ms. Trotter, please calm down and allow the girls to play."

"No! They need to come over here and fix this mess they done got me into!"

Bethany jotted more notes as the two girls trudged over.

"Yes, ma'am?" they said together.

"Why ya'll sit up here and lie to this lady like that, talking 'bout I'm always leaving y'all at home by y'all self!"

"I 'on't know," they answered, clearly intimidated by their mother's yelling.

"Now, you see that? You see that?" Feenie said, turning to Bethany. "They don't know! They 'bout to have me sittin' behind bars based on they don't know." She sucked her teeth and slammed her body back down on the bench. "Go'n and play," she ordered.

"Thank you for your time today, Ms. Trotter." Bethany pulled her messenger bag up on her shoulder after sliding her portfolio inside, then walked off to her car. "I will give you a follow-up call by week's end."

CHAPTER 19

Two weeks had passed with no deposit into her checking account, and Terryn wasn't having it. As she drove across the city making her final approach into Rance's neighborhood, she placed a call to his office, being sure to dial *67 first so her number wouldn't show on the caller ID system. As best she could, she disguised her voice once Rance answered.

"Rance Alexander," he said into the phone's mouthpiece.

"Oh, you think this is a game and a joke, huh? Well, we'll see who's going to be laughing in another hour." She snapped the phone closed and sped on the highway to 4403 Centera Lane, the home of the Alexanders.

Without a single nerve jumping out of place, Terryn stepped out of her car and practically stomped to the door. She pressed the doorbell and waited momentarily for Laiken to answer.

"Oh, hi, Terryn." Laiken beamed, already familiar with her from visiting Rance at work. "It's such a surprise to see you; my husband let you out of that zoo a little early today, huh?"

"Something like that." Terryn smiled cordially. "He actually let me out early several weeks ago, which is why I'm here. I wanted to talk to you about something."

"Oh, really?" Laiken instinctively braced herself, not sure what Terryn was going to say.

"Come on in. Can I get you something to drink?"

"Um . . . some water would be fine, please."

"Sure. I'll be right back." Laiken disappeared in the kitchen, picked up the phone, and dialed her husband's cell number, starting in on him as soon as he answered. "I don't know what is going on, but I didn't sign up for this crap!" she whispered.

"What's going on, Laiken?" Now that he'd told his wife the whole truth, he had no reason to react in fear or intimidation. While things were far from smoothed over, they'd blown over enough for him to at least spend the night in his own house, albeit that it had to be in the guest room, and that's where he'd been ever since.

"Terryn is sitting here in our living room and has come over wanting to talk to me."

"I'm on my way." Rance hung up the phone, gathered up his things, and tried to head out of the office, but was delayed once he realized he had a client sitting in the lobby area whom he'd pretty much forgotten about. He had no other choice but to meet with the gentleman, then head for home.

* * *

Laiken returned carrying a serving tray with two bottled waters and a cluster of grapes surrounded by squares of cheese, and two small saucers and forks. "So, what brings you by? I certainly wasn't expecting anyone from the office."

"Laiken, I've worked for your husband for a long time. And over the years, my heart has just gone out to you and all that you have gone through, knowingly or maybe unknowingly," Terryn started, placing a hand over her chest. "And it's just so unfair," she gasped, feigning sincerity, and taking her voice's octave up a notch. "I'm sorry, I'm sorry." Terryn fanned back imaginary tears.

"What is it?" Laiken asked.

"I just look at the way you carry yourself, so neat and poised and sophisticated, and I have to ask myself, what would make somebody do that?" Terryn took a swig of water, then continued with her act. "I just think the world of you and I look up to you so much for the way you stand by and support your husband the way you do."

Laiken popped a grape into her mouth along with a cube of cheese.

"And then for him to . . ." Terryn looked up at Laiken with eyes filled with remorse. "For him to cheat on you the way he has."

"Excuse me?"

"Laiken, your husband has children by another woman." Terryn reached for her purse and dug out photos of Feenie, Cara, and Mia, then offered them to Laiken.

Laiken took the photos and gulped as she saw the images of a black woman and two mixed children. Instantly, her eyes spilled the tears that could not be held back. While Rance had told her about his other "family," he hadn't let on that Feenie was black. Again she became infuriated. Just then Rance turned the knob of the front door and entered his home. Before he could get both feet in good, he'd caught a glimpse of Terryn sitting on his couch with a smug look on her face, but more importantly saw his wife charging at him like a raging bull.

"You didn't tell me the woman was black! Rance, how could you!" she shrieked, giving her best attempt to throw the photos in his face, but the paper was too light to do anything other than flutter to the floor. Rance closed the door and picked up the photos, while Laiken stood by waiting for some type of response from him. He recognized the photos as the same ones Terryn had mailed to him in his second and third cards.

"I didn't know how to tell you," he muttered. "Didn't think it would matter much anyway."

"I hate you!" Laiken spat. "You are nothing but a nasty, lying, cheating . . . bastard!" She wanted to use harsher words, but nothing she could have said would have expressed the anger she felt at the moment. "And why did you let me find out like this, Rance? Why?"

"Sit down, Laiken; Terryn, get out of my house," he instructed calmly.

"No! You sit right there. She's not going anywhere until I'm satisfied that all of your lies have been exposed. Please stay, Terryn," Laiken requested, stepping toward Terryn, motioning with her hands for her to stay seated.

"Do you know what this woman is doing, Laiken? You have her sitting here in our home, and she has been blackmailing me!"

"Ohhhhh! So now the truth comes out! So it wasn't about you wanting to embrace these children you call your daughters, it was really about you wanting to stop paying out money! You selfish son of a—"

"Laiken! I told you about this woman and the girls," he stated, shaking the photos at her before tossing them on the table. "I told you!" This bit of information shocked Terryn, not knowing that Rance had already confessed, but to her advantage Laiken bought her a little time to think.

"Well, you should have told me the whole story! After all, omission is just as good as lying! But you're an attorney, you know all about that, don't you?"

All Terryn needed was a box of popcorn and some Raisinets. Once Laiken became silent for a minute, Terryn spoke up. "Laiken, I wasn't blackmailing your husband. He offered to pay me money once I found out about his affair and the children."

"And just how did you find out?"

"Well, Jerrafine was just visiting the office a little too frequently and most of the time after hours," Terryn fabricated.

"That's a lie and you know it!" Rance yelled, but at this point he had absolutely no credibility with his wife.

"You shut up!" Laiken ordered, easily silencing Rance.

"I would see her coming in like right at the end

of the day when there were no more appointments scheduled and Mr. Alexander would always agree to see her. Always. Of course I became suspicious, especially given the way the woman would be dressed, which was just a couple of threads more than what a stripper would wear, or usually a trench coat and platform heels," Terryn continued. "It wasn't until one evening she'd come in near closing as usual, and I'd left but needed to return to get my purse, that my suspicions were confirmed. I came back into the office, but before I could leave again, I heard this loud crash from his office. Of course I rushed back there to see what was going on, and, Laiken, I was so embarrassed. I was so embarrassed by what I saw." Terryn paused, letting Laiken draw her own conclusion. "I was so shocked and stunned I couldn't even move, and when your husband realized I was standing there, right away he started begging me to keep it to myself and immediately increased my salary, which was more than two years ago," she lied.

Laiken glared at her husband, who glared at Terryn. Truth be told, he hadn't slept with Feenie since she'd gotten pregnant with the twins, but kept silent because there had been a few women that had visited his office after hours, and he could only pray that Terryn wouldn't magically pull out photos of them.

"Naturally I accepted the salary increase, but not all money is good money. I just felt so bad for you and your boys. And I will admit, I did get used to the extra money, but it was just eating away at my soul that I've been accepting this money to keep my mouth shut."

"Do you have proof of that?"

"All I have with me is my last month bank statement, where you can see that every single week, deposits of two thousand dollars were being made to me by his firm." She pulled a sheet of folded paper out of her purse and handed it to Laiken. "Now, here is my check stub, which has my regular pay on it, and there would be no other reason why Mr. Alexander would need to give me extra money if what I was telling you were not true," she stated, closing her case.

Laiken eyed the document, then tossed it on the table. Quickly Rance grabbed it, wanting to compare the account numbers and confirm that they indeed matched what had been sent to him in the cards, and what Pete had presented to him as Nadia's account information. Terryn didn't stop him, not knowing that he already knew the account was not in her name.

"And not only that," Terryn added, prepared to spill all the beans. "The only reason why he is coming clean with you now is that those girls' mother is in a position to lose the children. She was caught leaving them at home alone, and will probably have to serve time." Terryn had made sure to get the full story or as much of that story as she possibly could the day she arrived at Nadia's house and saw the police squad cars parked in front of Feenie's home. "If it wasn't for him having to take in the girls, he probably wouldn't have told you that at all." *Perfect*, she thought to herself.

"So, this is it, huh, Rance? You would have kept

this whole thing hidden but you might just have to take the girls in. Well, I'm prepared to offer you a plea bargain, sir," Laiken said sarcastically. "I will take those girls. They can come here and live and I will take great care of them," she hissed. "But instead of you paying this woman, you're going to pay me, because I'm going to take you for everything you got. And you're not just going to give me what you were giving her, you are going to double that because I know you've been forking money over to these children's mother. As a matter of fact, you're going to give me triple because I was stupid enough to have your sons and believe that you were faithful to me." She folded her thin arms across her chest. "Terryn, do you have any idea what my husband was paying to who is it? Jerrafine?" she guffawed in disgust.

"Actually I do."

Rance gasped.

Terryn pulled out a printed copy of the firm's Accounts Payable records, which showed amounts made payable to Jerrafine Trotter, and although it was several months old, it was recent enough to be believable. Rance could only shake his head.

"You need to leave," Laiken said to her husband after looking the documents over. "As a matter of fact, both of you get out of my house!" She jumped to her feet and scurried to the front door, holding it open for the both of them.

"I'm so sorry, Laiken," Terryn uttered as she passed her by. Feeling accomplished, she headed for her car, leaving Rance there to argue further with his wife. The only thing about it now was she didn't know how she was going to make ends meet and still needed a job.

CHAPTER 20

"In the case of the state of Maryland against Jerrafine Trotter, you are being found guilty for two counts of child neglect involving the minor children Carance Alexander and Mirance Alexander. You will appear back here on a later date for sentencing and will need to prepare to have your children cared for by a capable family member, or else they will be taken into custody by the state."

The remainder of what the judge had to say was just a blur to Feenie. Not just in words, but also in vision, as her eyes filled with tears. She turned to look at her mother, who sat just behind her for support.

"Don't worry about it. You'll get a suspended sentence," she told her daughter once they left. "It will be all right." Although she tried to offer words of comfort, she swayed Feenie away from asking her to take the girls in and coached her to allow their father to keep them.

"Mama, his wife don't even know these girls exist; he ain't gone take 'em," she muttered.

"Well, the least you can do is ask him. Because you don't want those girls to end up in foster care."

"Can't you take 'em?" Feenie blurted.

"Chile, you know I don't have no room in the house for them girls. And you know my job got me working these crazy hours all during the day and night. They wouldn't be no better off with me than they are right now with you."

"But, Mama, you know I don't have no other options," she whined. "I wouldn't be asking you if I didn't need it, Ma."

"I told you to ask those girls' father," her mother said with such finality, Feenie didn't comment again.

Once Feenie got home, she called Rance, defeated, and told him the news, this time sans the harsh and manipulative tone she'd used with him over the course of eight years. "I got to go to sentencing next week, and I don't know what's going to happen with the girls."

"I'll take them," Rance said, shocking Feenie.

"You'll what? You . . . but what about your wife?"

"She knows about the girls." Rance didn't go into any details, but ended the call, letting Feenie know that he would attend her sentencing and be ready to accept the girls that very day if things didn't work in her favor. He hung up the phone and headed for Nadia's house, hoping that she'd gotten in for the evening. After ringing her doorbell, he was greeted by a large man with a mixture of gray and black wavy hair.

"May I help you?"

"Rance Alexander. I'm here to see Nadia please."

"Come on in," Nadia's father offered, recognizing his name as the attorney that was looking into Nadia's identity fraud case. "My daughter hasn't gotten home from work yet, but she should be here in about ten minutes or so. What have you found out?" he asked, closing the door behind Rance.

"If it's all right with you, I'd rather wait until Nadia arrives. Client confidentiality. You understand," Rance suggested.

"Of course. Go ahead and make yourself comfortable while I give Nadia a call and see how close she is to getting here. She's been looking forward to hearing from you, hoping you can shed some light on this case." Before Aidan could get to the phone Nadia was stepping in the door.

"Mr. Alexander," she greeted with a smile. "Hey, Daddy." She kissed her father's cheek.

"I must have just shut the door in your face," Aidan chuckled. "Mr. Alexander just walked in."

"I hope you have some news for me," Nadia said, turning to Rance.

"Actually, I've made some interesting discoveries."

"Let me get you something to drink before I get seated," she offered.

"I'll get it, baby girl; go ahead and handle your business." Aidan strolled to the kitchen and began opening cabinets while Nadia slid out of her pumps and took a seat on the couch by Rance.

He pulled out a folder of various documents

that were accented with multiple colored high-lighters and sticky tabs. "Well, most of the accounts that now are in delinquent status were opened up in Copperas Cove, Texas. Do you know anyone there or from there?"

"No, not that I can think of."

"The billing address listed on all the accounts is a PO box, registered in your name of course, so I wasn't able to get a physical billing address." He showed her a sheet of paper with a PO box address scribbled on it while Aidan joined them with a few canned beverages and small glasses filled with ice. "Now, the culprit seems to do quite a bit of online shopping, so there are several purchases that trace back to a ship-to address, which oddly is to a movie theater in South Carolina."

"What part? That's where I'm from," Aidan volunteered.

"Well, here's the address," Rance offered, reading from his notes. "Cherrydale Cinemas . . . Pleasantburg Drive."

"That's not too far from where I live. I'm about ten minutes out from there."

"It's hard to tell from the purchases alone whether your culprit is a male or female. There were items such as dresses, men's suits, sneakers, video games, shoes, electronic purchases, cell phones, you name it purchased and shipped to this movie theater. I was able to get my hands on a roster of the employees there. Do any of these names look familiar?"

Nadia and Aidan perused the list together, not identifying any names that seemed even vaguely familiar. "I don't know any of these people," she said, scanning the more than fifty names.

"The only other thing I found was a three-bedroom apartment, in your name of course, out in Rockford, Illinois. The rent's been paid a year up, courtesy of the credit card also established in your name."

"What? Who is living there?"

"A couple by the name of Steven and Linda Logan." He handed her a photo of a smiling couple enjoying dinner at Red Lobster.

Nadia shook her head cluelessly. "Don't know who they are." She studied the picture a few seconds longer trying to recognize the faces.

"Well, at least we have a place to start. It won't be long before I'll have more information," Rance said confidently. "Then we can work on getting these things removed off your credit report." He left the folder on the table, and rose to his feet. "I'll be in contact as things progress."

"Thank you, Mr. Alexander."

"Call me Rance," he insisted as he reached for Aidan's hand. "Mr. Mitchell, nice meeting you. Wish it were under better circumstances."

"Likewise." Aidan saw Rance out, then turned toward his daughter, who still sat perplexed by the information in front of her.

"I don't know who these people are, Daddy." She scrutinized the picture of the couple carefully, while her mental Rolodex spun in rapid circles still trying to place the faces.

"Don't worry about it right now, sweetheart. Let's see what other information this attorney is able to turn up. In the meantime, don't we have a dinner date?"

"Yes, we do." Nadia winked. Together they headed out to have dinner with Jonathan and Lola. Just as they stepped out, Terryn cruised to a halt in front of the house. "Oh boy, Daddy. Help me to bite my tongue. How is she going to use my name to blackmail someone?" she uttered as Terryn stepped out onto the street.

"You'll do just fine, sweetie. Think of what's at risk if you tip her off."

With that said, Nadia pasted a smile on her face hoping that it would pass as genuine.

"Hey, girl!" Terryn called as she strode up the sidewalk. "I just came by to pick up something right quick. I think I left a pair of shoes under the bed."

"Oh, okay. No problem." Nadia reached in her bag for her keys.

"You better follow her," Aidan warned under his breath.

"Amen to that."

"Hey, Mr. Mitchell," Terryn said respectfully.

"How've you been, Terryn? Long time no see."

"Yeah, it has been a while. You're still looking good, I see," she teased.

"Yeah, still hoping that one day your mom will give me the time of day," he chuckled.

"Oh, you too late for that, she done jumped up and got married! Running around the country being a newlywed," she giggled, following Nadia into the house. In less than a minute, with a box tucked under her arm, she said her good-byes and sped off.

"Remind me to change your locks tonight. Does she have your alarm code?" Aidan asked, nodding his head toward the ADT sign planted in Nadia's yard.

"No, sirrrr!"

"That's my girl."

Lola Strickland opened Jonathan's door and immediately the smells of home cooking wafted into Nadia's and Aidan's nostrils. Nadia couldn't dectect what it was Jonathan's mother had prepared, but whatever it was made her ten times hungrier than she had been.

"How are you, Ms. Lola?" Nadia offered a loose hug as she passed through the doorway. "This is my dad, Aidan Mitchell."

"Good evening," Aidan said respectfully.

"And this is Jonathan," she introduced with a smirk, only because she was trying not to smile, but it didn't work—she couldn't help it.

"How are you doing, sir?" Jonthan asked, reaching for Aidan's hand.

"Great. Nice to meet you." Aidan's eyes scanned the walls and furnishings of Jonathan's home. "This is quite a place you have here," he commented.

"It's just like mine, Daddy."

"Oh, it is, isn't it?" Aidan nodded his head with new revelation. "Just looks a little different with a few man things in it, I guess."

"Thank you, sir," Jonathan replied with a head bob.

"Ms. Lola, it's smelling some kinda good in

here." Nadia rubbed her belly while trying to inconspicuously avoid Pazzo. That didn't work either.

"He ain't gone do nothing to you," Lola said, waving her hand in dismissal but all the while cutting her eyes at Jonathan as if to say, "Mmm-mm, don't let her have your babies."

"Oh yes, ma'am, I know," Nadia responded, letting out a nervous laugh, now feeling obligated to at least pat the dog's head or something. "Dad, isn't he . . ." Nadia looked up to say something to her father, but caught him twinkling eyes with Lola. *What in the world! I know my daddy ain't tryna get his mack on!*

"Huh?" he said, catching himself.

"Nothing; never mind." Whatever Nadia had been trying to form and say had been snatched from her mind.

"You two can wash your hands while Jonathan and I set the table," Lola instructed.

While Nadia was in the bathroom, she overheard Aidan talking to Jonathan. "So, what is it that you do again? You head some kind of global operation or something, right?"

"Yes, sir, that's exactly what I do."

"Are they paying you well for it?"

"I do all right," Jonathan replied.

"How long have you lived in this house?" *Deg, Daddy, slow it up a bit!* Nadia thought, only turning on a trickle of water so that she could hear the rest of the conversation.

"Just moved here earlier this year actually. I spend so much time on the road, sometimes I wonder why I should even have a home, but then again, you know what they say . . . there's no place like it," Jonathan finished.

"I have to agree with you on that one," Aidan said. Nadia emerged from the bathroom and took a seat at the dining room table while, one at a time, everyone else took to the bathroom.

Once they were all seated, Ms. Lola asked Jonathan to bless the food. He cleared his throat nervously and mumbled a few words that were barely audible. As soon as the group added an amen on the end and popped their eyes open, Ms. Lola embarrassed her son.

"Boy, I *know* you know how to pray better than that. I know you do. What kind of blessing we supposed to get out of that? All I gotta say is . . ." She looked over at Nadia and Aidan. "Y'all better be glad that I fixed this food myself, so y'all don't have to worry about no salmonella and E. coli and food poisoning, 'cause with that little baby prayer this grown man call hisself saying, wouldn't nothing be fit ta eat."

Nadia suppressed a snicker, although she was embarrassed for Jonathan, but he seemed not to mind it.

For the next hour, they feasted on the best meat loaf Nadia had ever had in her life, not that she'd had many past entrées to choose from, a fluffy and sweet carrot soufflé, macaroni and cheese, and fried cabbage. Aidan ate as if it were going to be his last meal before a forty-day fast, complimenting Ms. Lola every few seconds.

"I can't remember when I had a meal so good," he said, doing everything but lick his plate. He was grateful for a real meal. Being the single man that he was, dinners for him mostly consisted of something off the roasting rack at his neighborhood 7-Eleven, Chinese takeout, or a two-piece meal deal from Kentucky Fried Chicken. "Boy, if I had a woman that cooked like this for me every night . . . wooo-weee! I'd be a happy man," Aidan commented, smacking his lips.

Nadia shook her head in slight embarrassment. "Daddy, you just as country as a plaid couch sitting on the front porch for patio furniture." Both Aidan and Jonathan chuckled.

"Ain't nothing wrong with telling the truth. What was that you fixed me to eat last night? Some thawed-out meatballs sitting on a pile of rice with some canned gravy poured on top of it."

"You said it was good!" Now Nadia was almost mortified. She glanced at Jonathan, who hid his laughter behind a napkin. *He 'bout to have this man thinking I can't cook!* She nudged him under the table with a swing of her knee.

"It was good, baby girl—it just don't compare to this. This some good eatin' right here."

Lola giggled like a schoolgirl and batted her thin lashes. "Oh, hush on up, now. It's just all right," she said in false modesty. Jonathan stared at his blushing mother for a few seconds, then shook his head.

Just when Aidan thought he couldn't eat another bite, the oven went off. Lola opened its mouth and pulled out a baked dessert. "Is that a homemade apple cobbler?" Aidan piped up, almost ready to do cartwheels across the kitchen. "'Cause that shore don't look like nothing outta a box from the store shelf!"

"It ain't mucha nothing. Just something I threw together for y'all." She scooped healthy servings on plates, added a dollop of ice cream to each one, then brought them two at a time to the table.

And she was worried about ribs *killing somebody?* Nadia thought as she filled her mouth with the sinfully sweet mixture of both hot and cold desserts.

After they all ate until they could barely move, Nadia offered to help with the dishes, looking for Jonathan to be the one to respond.

"That would be so nice if you could take care of 'em for me, sweetie," Lola answered instead, sliding back from the table.

"Oh yes, ma'am; it's the least I could do after such a wonderful meal," she complimented as she began gathering plates from the table, expecting Jonathan to rise and join her. Much to her chagrin, Jonathan followed their parents into the living and took a seat on the couch.

Nadia's jaw nearly hit the floor. *Oh no, he didn't!* she thought. *He done went in there and sat his rusty, dusty, apron-string-holding behind on the couch and got me standing at the sink washing one hundred and one dishes all by myself! He knows he supposed to be in here helping me—not sitting in there rubbing his belly like he's some kinda black Buddha!* Fuming the entire time, Nadia decided to finish the job to save face, although with the swipe of each dish she was tempted to quit. "That's what I get for offering in the first place," she mumbled. "I ain't no doggone Molly maid!"

While she scrubbed dish after dreaded dish, her thoughts slowly turned from what she secretly named the Three Trifling Gluttons in the living room, her daddy included, to whom it could have been living high on the hog on her ticket. She was certain that she didn't know any Steves, or Lindas, or Logans. At least not that she could remember. Nadia knew plenty of people in South Carolina from her hometown, but no names on that roster popped out to her. She was just anxious to get to the bottom of it, sue the pants off somebody, and restore her credit.

Just as Nadia dried and put away the last pan, Jonathan came waltzing in with his hands stuffed into the pockets of his starched khakis. "Well, if it ain't the mama's boy himself," she said under her breath.

"Want me to help you?"

"Help me what?" she spat lowly, cutting her eyes so sharp at him she was actually surprised he didn't just start bleeding. He had the nerve to chuckle. "Ain't nothing funny."

"You look good in the kitchen," he poked. Nadia rolled her eyes in response. Jonathan walked over and leaned against the counter beside the sink. "My mama and your daddy in there trying to make out," he whispered. "I think they are going for a walk; that is what they were talking about when I got out of there."

"Humph!" Nadia grunted. Sure enough, a few seconds later the front door opened and Aidan and Lola were calling out, "We'll be back!"

And as soon as that door shut, Nadia was ready to beat Jonathan down, but held on to herself. Instead she decided to try to find out whether she had passed Lola's scrutiny.

"So, what did your mom have to say about me?" she started.

He shrugged. "She hasn't said much of anything."

"She had to say something. I mean, she didn't share her first impression with you or nothing?" Nadia dug.

"Not really."

She didn't believe him because he wouldn't look directly at her. A few seconds of silence passed.

"You're lying," Nadia suddenly accused, looking him straight in the eye. "She just doesn't like me and you don't want to say that." Her hands flew to her hips as she stepped forward in Jonathan's face. His silence confirmed what she'd concluded, and that's when Nadia's dam broke. "See I should have known that any man who would let his mama break up his relationship is not worth my time."

"Break up my relationship? What are you talking about?" Jonathan asked, crinkling his brow.

Nadia sucked in a tiny gasp, realizing that she'd put her foot in her mouth and at the same time spilled her own personal beans about rambling through his things. Nonetheless, she tried to lie her way out. "Because you sat up there and told me!"

Jonathan didn't buy it. "I have never told you that," he said calmly, folding his arms across his chest.

Nadia stood silent for a few seconds until she reasoned that she might as well keep going since she'd let the cat out the bag. "Okay, so I read it in your journal! But you know what, I found out a whole lot about you, you . . . mama's boy!" she hurled. "So what you got a big fat paycheck? I wouldn't want no man who wears a size-large condom but his mama got him by the balls and controls everything he does! And then you screwing around with that tramp down the street who don't know how to keep her kids, and you expect me to just take you up on dinner just 'cause you asked?"

"Wow," he said calmly with a few head bobs. "Wow." He nestled his chin in the webbing between his thumb and index fingers, then lightly tapped his cheek.

"And then you have the nerve to be bipolar. What the hell am I thinking even coming over here for you to mess around and snap on me and my daddy? You crazy as a bedbug and I'm sitting here worried about what your mama thinks of me—why should I even care?"

"Bipolar?" Jonathan began to snort and snicker until he was doubled over in full-blown laughter. "What in the world did you find that gave you that impression?" he managed to say as puffs of laughter rose from his belly and tumbled out of his wide-open mouth.

"I saw that medicine bag thing with the toothpaste in it upstairs!" Nadia yelled.

This made Jonathan laugh even harder. "I don't know what you're talking about."

"Yes, you do," she shot, throwing the dish towel down on the countertop. "You know full well what I'm talking about. That little travel kit with the name of that crazy schizophrenic drug on the outside of it."

"Ohh!" he said, suddenly identifying with what Nadia was talking about. "You're talking about that little toiletry travel kit. My sister gave me that when she was working at a doctor's office," he explained. "The pharmaceutical salespeople give away stuff like that all the time. You probably have an ink pen or two right in your house."

Nadia momentarily studied his face for truth, bouncing her eyes back and forth between his. "Oh." That was all she could think of to say after pondering on his words for a few seconds more. "Well, you still let your mom control your life," she added, struggling for a new angle.

"And you've got bad credit," he retorted. "Now which one of those is worse? A man who cherishes his mother, or a woman who gotta get a payday loan because she would get rejected at the bank?"

Nadia gasped so loud, she practically inhaled all the air in the room while both her hands flew to her mouth, then dropped to her sides. "What! No, I don't! Well, actually now I do, but it's not my fault," she defended.

"What do you mean? There isn't a single bill you owe that you didn't at some point sign your name in ink for," he said knowingly with raised eyebrows. "So how is your bad credit not your fault? What—you got a husband somewhere that ran up your bills before you divorced?" Jonathan asked facetiously.

"No! Someone stole my identity, if you have to know so bad!"

Jonathan bit into his bottom lip and this time studied her face before speaking. "Well, ain't that something?" he asked with a slight guffaw. "You go through every nook and cranny of my house while I'm away, think I'm stupid enough not to notice, and then get offended when I ask *you* a question." He shook his head.

"I . . . I . . ." Nadia wanted to say she hadn't gone through every nook and cranny of his house, and actually she hadn't, but she'd been through enough to just not say anything else other than "I'm sorry, Jonathan. I'm really sorry." Embarrassed and ashamed, she grabbed her purse off the table in the hallway and exited as quickly as she could. Jonathan didn't move to stop her. He stood perfectly still for close to a minute replaying the conversation that had led up to Nadia's rushing out. He could have kicked himself for the words he couldn't take back, wishing he would have handled the situation differently. He thought about the way her hair swung about her shoulders as she bobbed her head in frustration, and the way her lips, though puckered in anger, were positioned for a smooth and flawless kiss.

"It's water under the bridge now," he said, looking at Pazzo. "Come on and eat, man," he called out to the canine, filling his dish with food, then taking a seat at the table, blankly watching him eat.

He thought how Lola really hadn't warmed up to Nadia, and how it disappointed him. He was hoping that for once someone that he had an interest in Lola would actually find halfway suitable. "So what if she bought takeout? I eat out all the time anyway." Pazzo looked up at his master for only a split second, as if to acknowledge what

Jonathan had said, but then dipped his head back into his feeding dish. "And I love ribs, beef, or pork," he continued. A part of him wanted to cross the street and make up with Nadia, but his feet seemed to be cemented to the floor, and his behind to the chair. "Me and Mama gone have to talk about some things."

Being the true gentleman that he was, Aidan walked Lola to Jonathan's front door and lightly pecked her cheek.

"I got to tell you again, Lola, that was some kinda meal you cooked up today."

"I'm glad you enjoyed it. I don't get to cook like that much anymore now that my kids are grown, gone, and on their own. I miss it some kinda bad too."

"Well, maybe before I leave, I can convince you to fix up some chicken and dumplings and a pecan pie," Aidan tested. "I'll buy the stuff."

"I think I can squeeze that in sometime next week. How long you here for?"

"I was planning on going back to South Carolina next Tuesday. How 'bout you?"

"I fly out next Friday, so I can definitely fix that up for you."

"Your place or mine?" Aidan asked with a wink.

"We'll see, 'cause I 'on't want no mess if I come over there, now," Lola teased back. "You look like you still got some man in ya."

Aidan let out a hearty laugh. "I'm always gone have that, Lola." He extended his finger to press the doorbell. "Always. You look like you still got some hot mama in—"

"It's about time you two teenagers made it back here," Jonathan said, swinging the door open and cutting Aidan off midsentence. "How was your walk?"

Lola was still blushing from what Aidan had attempted to say. "It was quite nice. Nice indeed."

"Good. Come on in, Mr. Mitchell."

"Nah. I think I best be headin' on back across the street. Nadia still here?" Aidan asked, peering around Jonathan just a bit.

"No. She left about forty minutes ago. Shortly after you two went out for some night air."

"Oh, okay. Well, let me get on over there, put my feet up, and sleep off the food that didn't get walked off just now. It was nice meeting you, young man." Aidan extended his hand for a firm shake.

"Likewise. I enjoyed having you over."

"We gone have to sit down and talk like men before I leave next week."

"Absolutely. Yes, sir," Jonathan agreed, not knowing whether Aidan wanted to talk about his own interest in Lola, or Jonathan's interest in his daughter.

"G'night, Miss Lola. Thank you again for a wonderful evening."

"My pleasure. Good night to you, now."

No sooner had the door closed and been locked than Lola started in on Nadia. "Let me go in here and see what kind of job this girl done did in here with these dishes." With quick steps she strode down the hallway in Jonathan's kitchen. Jonathan folded his lips into his mouth and followed his mother. As if she had on a white inspection glove, Lola began checking the sink, the countertops, and other surfaces.

"Mama, what are you doing?" Jonathan asked, leaning back against the refrigerator.

"I'm tryna see if this girl knows how to clean up. I done told you this before, you don't want no woman that's gone keep a nasty house. You want somebody that know how to keep the house clean. A chaste housekeeper is what you need."

"I can determine that on my own, Ma."

"I know you can, but sometimes the mama can see stuff that the child cain't see until it's too late. And you can believe this—your mama got your best interests at heart, baby."

"I know you do, Mama, but I also need you to recognize that I'm a full-grown man, capable of making my own decisions."

"Oh, I know you grown. I ain't disputin' that, but you gone always be my baby too, now," she reminded her son. "And somma these women need a mother to check them out before we just let them up and marry our young men."

"Mama, nobody said anything about marriage."

"Not yet you didn't, but if you keep on hanging round somebody, that's gone sooner or later pop out them lips of yours. Now, you best let me check up on these little fast-tail girls 'fore you get too involved. 'Cause the wrong one will come up in here and take everything you got and leave your poor ol' mama with nothing."

"Is that what this is about? You scared somebody is going to take something away from you?"

Jonathan had hit the nail right on the head,

but Lola wouldn't admit it. "Naw! That ain't it at all. I just don't wanna see you with somebody who don't mean you no good."

"That, or you don't want to see me with anyone who you think poses a threat to you and your extracurricular spending habits?"

Lola gasped. "How dare you say something like that to me? I ain't never done nothing but love you and raised you up to be a fine young man. But now you done got a little bit above yourself. You done got a little bit too big for them boxers you wear."

"Mama, cut it out."

"Cut it out? Cut what out, Jonathan? Cut what out? Here I am, breaking my back to make sure that you taken care of, and all you—"

"Make sure I'm taken care of? You sure it's me you're thinking about? I think you are more interested in making sure *you* are taken care of!"

"Who are you taking that tone with, Jonathan Pernell Strickland?" Lola asked, her voice beginning to quiver. "I'm still your mama, you know!"

"And you always will be, but you cannot continue to run my life, Mama. I'm a grown man. I know how to pick a mate, contrary to your belief. Now, I let you mess things up for me in the past with other interests that I had, but I can't do that anymore. I won't do it," Jonathan said with finality.

Lola stood stunned for a few seconds, the shock apparent in her expression. "Well, fine. Fine! Just forget about me altogether, then," she said, bursting into tears. "Don't you worry 'bout me no more!"

"Okay, and here you go with your manipulative

tricks." Jonathan verbally acknowledged his recognition of this tactic.

"Manipulative?" Lola gasped. "I resent you saying that."

"Resent it as you may, Mama, it's true. You will do and say anything to get your way, and I usually give in to your pleas, but not anymore."

"Some old hot-tailed floozy comes flaunting in here and now—"

"Nadia is not a floozy, so cut it out. Cut it out!" he repeated. "I am the only child you have that you read this riot act to. The only one. You don't do this to Adonna, Stephanie, or Diane. And you know why you don't? Because they don't have any money to offer you." Once Jonathan spoke those words, he felt as if he'd been released from a debtor's prison.

"I don't want your money, Jonathan. I don't want a dime from you," Lola tried to defend. "I thought you did stuff for me because you loved me, but I see better now."

"And I still do love you. You know that. You are going to always be my mother, and I'm going to always be your son. That does not mean that you can control my life or my checkbook."

Lola snorted loudly, still in tears. "It's all right. Go'n and live your life. Y'all probably plan on putting me in an old folks' home soon anyway. Probably just gone leave me there to rot and die."

"I have heard enough of this." Jonathan turned away and started toward the front door.

"Don't you walk away when I'm talking to you, boy!" she shouted behind him, then followed with quick steps.

"Come on, Pazzo," Jonathan called out while he reached in his front closet for the dog's leash. "I'll be back when you get yourself together." He snapped the leash onto Pazzo's collar. "And I mean what I said, Mama. You can cry and throw a fit all you want. I love you and you know that. I'm gonna always love you—that don't mean you get everything you want." Jonathan leaned forward to press his lips to his mother's cheek, then exited with his dog, leaving Lola standing there sniveling and bewildered.

CHAPTER 21

It was a sad day. Rance helped the two crying girls climb into his Silverado with several of their things in the back. Feenie had been sentenced to serve sixteen months in the local jail, and her mother refused to take the twins in. Rance had already prepared Laiken, David, and Michael that at the very least, the girls would be coming to spend a few occasional weekends, but could possibly be coming to live. David and Michael were ecstatic about having more kids to play with, twins at that. Laiken, of course, was a harder case, but had ultimately decided to try to work through things, once Rance committed to counseling. Even so, most days she was in a foul mood and barely spoke to her husband.

Rance knew it would be a rough road, but felt good about having his girls in his home. They drove across the town and into Ellicott City, then pulled into the driveway of Rance and Laiken's lavish five-bedroom home.

"Wow!" Mia and Cara both exclaimed with stretched eyes.

"This is where you girls will be living for a while," Rance said, looking over his shoulder at his daughters and, for the first time that day, noticed a hint of a smile. As the girls tumbled from the vehicle's backseat, Laiken came out to greet them and showed them to their bedroom, as much as it hurt her ego. The girls gave a respectful hello with a slight smile, but smiled even more once they viewed their room, expertly decorated in pink and white, with two single beds and a vanity for the both of them. The girls' eyes popped wide open in awe, absorbing their new surroundings.

"So, do you like it?" Rance asked, bringing bags of new clothes Laiken had purchased for the twins the week before anticipating what they might need.

"We love it!" Cara answered, spinning in two full circles with her head thrown back and arms extended to the side. Mia quickly followed suit. In seconds the girls were giggling as they both landed in a heap on the floor. "Daddy, which one of the beds is mine?" Mia asked.

"Do I get to choose, or do you want to do it?"

"You pick, you pick!" the girls chanted, jumping up and down.

"Okay, then . . ." Rance playfully covered his eyes with his hands, turned in a single circle, then with his eyes still closed, pointed with his left hand to the right. "This one is for Mia"— then pointed with his right hand to his left— "and this one's for Cara."

"Yeah!" they both yelled as they dove on their beds. "Thank you, Daddy!"

Laiken cringed on hearing these foreign children refer to her husband as daddy. It took all her strength not to walk out right then, but somehow she stayed, lifting the bags that Rance had brought in and walking them to the closet to begin hanging their clothes.

"I'll help you," Cara offered. "We do this all the time at my mama's house." She sprang to her feet and walked over to Laiken's side, catching her by surprise.

"Me too," Mia joined. Like two mini professionals the girls positioned the garments neatly on hangers, then reached over their heads to hang them on the closet's rack.

"Wow! You girls are really good at this, huh?" Laiken was impressed. She looked over at Rance, who simply shrugged his shoulders. When it came to her boys, she'd always folded and put away or hung their clothing up for them. To see the girls do it for themselves was both refreshing and amusing to Laiken. She had to admit to herself that the girls were quite beautiful. "I'm going to have to have you ladies show those rowdy boys how to do this."

"Okay—it's easy," Mia replied. "All they have to do is get their clothes out of the dryer, and then put their pants on a clippy hanger, and put their shirts on this kind of hanger." She held a plastic tube hanger in her hand, displaying it to Laiken. "Then they should put their socks in one drawer, and their T-shirts in another drawer, and their panties in another drawer."

Laiken burst into full laughter, which was something she hadn't done since she first heard of the girls' existence. Still laughing, she backed

herself into Rance's arms and he leaned downward to kiss her cheek.

"What's so funny?" Mia asked, perplexed.

"Nothing, sweetheart," Laiken answered,
trying to pull herself together. "I will finish that
up, you girls can go out to the backyard; Michael
and David are out there waiting for you with
water guns." With a shriek the girls headed for
the front door, not yet familiar with the layout of
the house, leaving Laiken and Rance standing in
their new bedroom.

Rance turned his wife to face him. "Laiken, I
know this is hard for you, but I very humbly thank
you." He paused, staring into his wife's eyes. "I realize that my apologies are not enough, my begging forgiveness probably cannot be honored,
but I am ever so grateful that you're opening up
our home and your heart to these girls." Laiken
could only nod as she patted her husband's
shoulder twice. "And I love you for that," he said.

Those weren't exactly the words that Laiken
wanted to hear at the moment. They were hard to
accept along with the fact that her husband had
been unfaithful, and now she'd be reminded of
that unfaithfulness every single day. While Rance
stating his love didn't hurt things, it didn't really
help either.

Without warning, tears began to trail down
her face. "This hurts, Rance," she said calmly.
"It hurts more than you could ever imagine."

Rance kept silent. He'd apologized a million
times before but knew the apologies didn't make
pain go away.

"I'll be in the kitchen." Laiken pulled away from

Rance's light embrace and headed toward the kitchen to start on dinner for her new extended family.

Not knowing what else to do, with random thoughts chasing each other in his mind, Rance led himself to the backyard and joined his four children. He found them sitting on the deck swapping different stories about school, movies, toys, and video games, using the water guns to drink from rather than spray each other. Sneaking up on the unsuspecting crew, Rance burst forward with a yell, equipped with the water hose on full blast. In an instant the kids screamed and scattered, looking for cover and firing back at their dad.

Rance spent the next hour horsing around the backyard, remembering again what it was like to be a kid. "All right, gang. I'll be inside," he announced, leaving the children outside to enjoy the rest of the evening sun. By the end of the day, Rance's sons and daughters had meshed together in friendship.

Home from work early, Nadia had barely made it in the door before her phone began to ring. She groaned at the sound, now accustomed to it being someone demanding from her money that she didn't owe. The constantly ringing phone almost made being at home unbearable.

She decided to ignore it, distracted by a wonderful aroma coming from the kitchen. "I know my daddy ain't cooked nothing," she commented to herself as she walked over to the stove. A large pot held the delectable chicken and dumplings Aidan had requested Lola to make.

By the time Aidan had come in the night he and Nadia had dinner at Jonathan's, Nadia had already thrown herself in bed and pretended to be asleep. While she was anxious to find out what had transpired on the walk her dad took with Lola, she was too upset over the conversation she and Jonathan had had to do any talking, so she did the next best thing. She pretended to be asleep, even when Aidan came peeking in her bedroom wanting to chat.

The following morning, Nadia met him at the breakfast table, where he sat sipping a cup of black coffee and reading the newspaper clad in a pair of navy blue pajamas, a plaid robe, black socks, and a pair of slippers.

"You look just like an old man, Daddy."

"I might look old, but don't let this look fool you none. Your daddy still got it," he bragged.

"Yeah, you need to tell me about that. What was with all that flirting and carrying on last night?"

"Aw, shucks, wa'n't nobody flirtin'; you making that up." Aidan grinned behind his paper.

"No, I'm not either. You were making googley eyes all night long at that woman." Nadia poured herself a cup of juice, warmed a cinnamon bagel, then joined Aidan at the table.

He shrugged. "What's wrong with having a little attention? Don't sit up here and act like you wa'n't cutting eyes back and forth across the table with that fella."

"I can't deny that, but we aren't talking about me right now, Daddy; we talking about you!"

Aidan chuckled. "I just told you, girl, I'm not as old as you think I am."

"All right, now. Don't hurt nobody." Nadia giggled with her dad.

"She s'posed to be coming over here next week and fixin' something to eat."

"What? You done talked that woman into coming over here and cooking? Yeah, you must still got it!" she teased.

Now today, Nadia was glad that Aidan had whatever it was that he still had. She couldn't have been hungrier than if she had eaten nothing more than rice cakes all day. She pulled down a plate from the cabinet and began filling it with Lola's prepared vittles. Peeking into a second pot, she found succulent butter beans complete with a large piece of pork seasoning nestled in its midst. "Pork?" she questioned. "What a hypocrite," she mumbled. Squares of buttery corn bread sat in a small basket covered with a paper towel. She added a couple to her plate, then took a seat at her dining room table, wondering where Aiden was as his car hadn't been in the driveway when she arrived. "He knows his way around," she dismissed, and dug into her food.

Twenty minutes later, Nadia trod up the steps, her belly full like it had been a few days back when Jonathan had them over. She reached the top landing, rounded the railing, and stopped in her tracks as without warning, the bathroom door swung open, exposing Lola wrapped in a towel with Aidan standing directly behind her with water running from his graying hair surrounded by a cloud of steamy fog.

"Oh Lawd!" Lola grabbed at her chest, then tightened the towel in embarrassment. Nadia stood frozen in place like a deer in headlights. Even though her mouth was wide open, no words would come forth.

"Hey, baby girl," Aidan finally said although equally embarrassed. "'Scuse us." He grabbed Lola's hand and led her to the spare bedroom as if it were nothing. "Come on, Lola."

With stretched eyes, Nadia looked on while the two seniors padded into the bedroom and closed the door. Had she not seen it with her own two eyes, Nadia would never have believed it. It took her next to a minute to pull herself together, as she couldn't even remember what it was she'd come upstairs for. Still in disbelief, and partially humored, she retraced her steps to go back to the lower level, grabbed her cell phone, and headed out of the front door. In a matter of seconds, she had Jonathan on the phone.

"You will never guess what I just saw," she said deliberately once Jonathan answered.

"A cow jumping over the moon?" he joked.

"Almost. Are you busy right now?" she asked, remembering he hadn't ended his workday.

"I have a few minutes."

"Okay. I get home, right? Your mama done came over there, cooked up a storm—some chicken and dumplings, butter beans, and corn bread—so I'm, like, cool! I fix me a little plate and eat. The food is delicious and all that. So then I go upstairs tryna make it to my room and guess who I catch coming out of the bathroom half naked?"

"Your daddy?" Jonathan guessed.

"And your mama!" she threw in.

"What!"

"I caught my daddy and your mama coming out of the bathroom together after they'd just gotten out of the shower."

Jonathan began chuckling.

"Ain't that a mess?"

"What did they say?"

"They didn't say anything. My daddy talking 'bout 'hey, baby girl, 'scuse me.' Then took your mama by the hand and went on into the bedroom like they married!"

"Well, they might not be married, but they sure are grown. But listen, I have to get back to work, okay? I'll give you a call later—or maybe I can stop by for some leftovers, if your daddy hasn't eaten them all by then," Jonathan guffawed.

It wasn't until Nadia got off the phone that she realized she wasn't supposed to be speaking to Jonathan.

Nadia rode over to Terryn's new place with the radio tuned to the Michael Baisden show, although she barely listened. Jonathan sat beside her wishing he could read her mind. He reached over and pushed a few strands of hair out of her face, evoking a slight smile.

"Is your mom still not speaking to you?" she asked.

"She'll be all right," he commented. He dug through a few CD cases in the armrest of Nadia's car and pulled out Mary J. Blige's latest, and slid the CD into the player. "This is what I said to my mama." He smirked, thumbing to Mary and Ludacris's track "Grown Woman," and began to sing. "Now, who you talkin' to, baby? I'm grown; now, who you talkin' to, baby? I'm grown!" Nadia had to laugh. She puckered her lips and danced as best she could being seating in the driver's seat and controlling a vehicle. She piped in when Mary sang the chorus.

"Tell your mama that you in love with a grown woman!" she sang. "Tell me the story again," Nadia begged. As if she hadn't heard it before, she listened intently while Jonathan did a short- ened version recap of the conversation he'd had with his mother before she'd left town . . . and again after Nadia caught her in her birthday suit.

"I just had to help her understand that I wasn't going to let her run off anyone else in my life. I had to set some boundaries, and she's not going to like them, but she's going to have to respect them and live with them."

Nadia smiled.

"And that comment you made about my mom having me by the balls, that kinda did something to a brotha." They both burst into laughter.

Before the song ended, they pulled up in front of Terryn's house.

"Come on in! I'm so glad y'all decided to pay a sister a visit." She threw her arms around her friend, then around Jonathan in greeting. "Where y'all coming from, spending some of your daddy's money, or your man's money?"

Nadia ignored Terryn's comment completely. Once she was made aware that it was Terryn who had ruined her financially, she thought long and hard about why she would have done such a thing. Then she suddenly realized how many times Terryn had made reference to her relationship with Aidan, and how she wished she had a father that would come to her rescue.

After she'd discussed this with Aidan, they both concluded that Terryn had become jealous and envious, watching her best friend enjoy life in a way that she hadn't been able to. Yet Terryn's betrayal made Nadia sick to her stomach.

"Your place is nice!" Nadia commented, checking out the décor upon entering. "Girl, wherever you work now, they must be really paying you well at your new job!"

"Yeah, I lucked up on a little something," Terryn bragged.

"Well, too bad you're not going to be able to keep it," Nadia stated flatly, taking a seat on Terryn's tan and burgundy Broyhill couch.

"What do you mean? I'm never leaving here."

"Oh, I don't think so."

"What makes you say that?" Terryn sat on the couch and offered Jonathan a seat. "You can come on in here, I don't bite."

"I'm good, thank you," Jonathan declined politely.

"Suit yourself," she dismissed with a wave of her hand. "Now, what are you talking about?"

"Terryn, I know," Nadia said, amazingly keeping her calm.

"You know what?" Terryn munched on a handful of microwave popcorn and stretched her eyes wide with curiosity.

Nadia reached into her tote bag and pulled out a thick folder of incriminating evidence. "I know that your mom married a man named Steven Logan, and for a wedding gift you set them up in an apartment in Rockford, Illinois." She opened the folder so Terryn could see a picture of her mom and stepdad sitting on the top of the documents. "I know that you took a trip to Texas last year and filled out at least five credit card applications using my personal information." She pushed through the stacks of statements and pictures, spreading them out on Terryn's glass coffee table. "I know your sister, Jessica Campbell-Stallings, works at the movie theater down in South Carolina, where you've been sending all your online purchases, then having her reroute them to you."

Nadia stood to her feet and waltzed to Jonathan's side while Terryn sat paralyzed, holding her breath. "I know you blackmailed Rance and had him send money to an account you set up in my name from the library. Look through there, there's a great shot of you using the WaMu ATM on Charles Street. And I know that as of tomorrow, you will be placed under arrest for extortion and identity fraud."

Terryn's mouth hung open as she grappled for words that would not come. "Nadia, wait; let me at least tell you what happened."

"That won't be necessary. Save that for your lawyer . . . if you can afford one." She turned on her heel and headed for Terryn's front door. "And like you told Rance's wife, not all money is good money."